FRANCES
AND HER GHOSTS

Rebecca Hughes Hall

Published by
Legend Press
51 Gower Street
London WC1E 6HJ

in association with
Five Seasons Press

Copyright © Rebecca Hughes Hall 2024

The right of Rebecca Hughes Hall to be identified as the author of this work has been asserted in accordance with the Copyright, Designs and Patents Act 1988. British Library Cataloguing in Publication Data available.

PRINT ISBN 9781917163583
EBOOK ISBN 9781917163590

All rights reserved. No part of this publication may be reproduced, stored in or introduced into a retrieval system, or transmitted, in any form or by any means (electronic, mechanical, photocopying, recording or otherwise), without the prior written permission of the publisher. This book is sold subject to the condition that it shall not be resold, lent, hired out or otherwise circulated without the express prior consent of the publisher.

Typeset in 12.5 on 16 Arno
at Five Seasons Press HR1 2QH UK

In the gutter of the market place of an Eastern town lay a dead dog, to the disgust of the passers-by. They called out their abuse at him. Then a gentle, rebuking voice broke in on the chorus of calumny, saying, 'Pearls are not equal to the whiteness of its teeth.' And the people drew away, whispering, 'Surely that must be Jesus, for who else would say a good word for a dead dog?'

Told on ancient tablets and re-told by the poet Nizami

If we know, then we must fight for your life as though it were our own ... for if they take you in the morning, they will be coming for us that night.

James Baldwin

Anti-Semitism is the same as delousing.

Himmler to the Waffen SS at Kharkov, 1943

Cruelty relies upon a rigid observance of the categorical distance between victim and oppressor.

Carol Lansbury

Prologue

'Come on, come on,' I called as I ran across the grass damp and dark with late evening, you running with me. I was running fast; the adrenaline was still flowing. I held you on the lead, but you strained at it, needing to feel movement in your limbs, and I could not match your eager speed. I think we were both hysterical, wound to breaking, breathing deep to regain ourselves. Then you stopped to investigate something interesting to dogs and stooping down, I looked into your face. It was very beautiful: your coat was smooth and black. Of medium height, you were of mixed breed – perhaps there was some Labrador in you? Your dark brown eyes had an earnest longing in them, as if you were pleading for human attention – or some recognition of your attempts to communicate with us. Your black nose was dry. The restraint was too much for both of us. In a moment of madness, I decided you should be free to run. I was sure you wouldn't leave me. We communicated heart to heart. Besides, I had biscuits in my pocket which you devoured with the abandoned relish of the hungry. I slipped the catch and you were free to dart about at a dog's pace. Then I panicked as your blackness disappeared into the blackness of the night when an exciting smell distracted you. I called, 'Here boy'. Seeing what I'd done, the others waiting nearby barely held their anger. It had to go somewhere.

We had just come through the gates of hell and its tangible presence was still with us. Who could leave it and forget? The smell was in our noses – a chemical and animal smell. But worse, was the sick stench of fear.

I would not turn to see the narrowed eyes or tightened lips. I refused to hear the curses hurled at me, but meant for the devils who, dressed in white on which redness of blood shows brightest, shadowed our minds. The white drill cotton cuffs which frame the white, fat, bony, red or brown hands, the fingers hair-lined to the wrists flexed to kill: I have seen them, in the daylight drinking tea from china cups almost daintily as if they were quite ordinary. Smiling with their mouths, their eyes dull, their hands many-shaped, like their words, manipulate; needles and knives sharp as their eyes precision-made to devour you. You disappear. Mysteriously.

But I managed to keep the calm of faith in you. We had already chosen each other. I whistled, waited, breath held to listen more acutely. I didn't answer the others, but walked some steps away from their anxiety. I whistled again, heart thumping, every muscle taut.

Then, at the third whistle, you came bounding back. You didn't have a name.

And I didn't want to impose one on you on our first meeting in case it confused you, for obviously someone had already claimed that privilege and your brain somewhere recalled its familiarity as if in a dream for the waking.

I held back the thought. The renting of ties and affection is our constant human fear. Dogs also mourn, and cows, sheep, pigeons, elephants, horses, primates. Remember them.

Your clouded history echoed back to me memories of many a sad parting, because I could not understand limitlessness and the strength of love to overcome.

'Here boy,' I called in a loud whisper. I waited, listening, barely breathing. I did not shout for fear of attracting attention. Then you caught up with me and leapt up in spontaneous acknowledgement of our friendship, I spun around as you leapt, feeling your muscles, stretching your limbs. You ran ahead, then, looking back, put your head down and came bounding back towards me, your smooth, lithe body easily covering the distance in seconds. Leaping up in a familiar greeting, you turned and ran ahead again. This you repeated several times. Months of pent-up energy burst into your every sinew and stretched you to the limits of your speed.

I picked up a stick from the ground and threw it. You ran after it and returned with it, and as I took it from your mouth, you gave it up with no playful protest. You had obviously done this kind of thing before. Someone had taught you to play with them on walks you took together.

I threw it again and you ran towards it, picked it up, then dropped it as an interesting scent caught your attention, and then another and another. You darted here and there as if you could not experience enough of the sensation all around you. I watched, sharing in your excitement.

Then you suddenly remembered me. I'd almost caught up with you and looking round you took off in a wide circle, before returning to be stroked. You stood still, panting with eager expectancy. An excited 'Go on then' sent you running, sniffing and leaping once again. No thought of the past spoiled your joy. No doubt for the future restrained one moment of it.

I watched as you rolled in the grass, then got up and shook yourself in that dog way that no human body can imitate, every muscle loosened for the first time in how long? Or did they keep to the rules and give you 'regular and suitable exercise'? What travesty of a concept of the natural world lived in their minds? Or perhaps they had none.

The prisons we make originate in our own minds. How we like to divide and contain everything. As if Creation's infinity could ever be contained!

The bars of your cage were the barriers in man's mind. Dogs have no such false concepts. You spoke most eloquently without words as, suddenly still, we faced one another.

That first, sweet smell of your fur after you had rolled in the grass heavy with the moisture of a late evening, was our bonding. You trusted me immediately. I wanted this newfound joy to last forever. Kneeling down, my head upon your slightly bowed head, I breathed deeply, your mouth open, showing your strong, white teeth as if you were smiling at freedom.

Those were your moments, fine moments in which Nature herself held you in her all-pervading arms and blotted out the memory of that place that was put only by minutes into the past.

When you gently licked my face, your paws around my neck, my arms around your back, there was a friendship so deep and so instant that it seemed as if it must well up from some mysterious source.

Yet amidst all this boisterous excitement, there was a calm about you. In your dark brown eyes I saw in those few still moments, a nobility, not merely of the stoic, but more, of a soul that has swallowed the poison of evil and transformed it through acceptance into something which reaches beyond our understanding.

I saw in those moments how troubled we humans are. We had snatched you from other humans who would trap you in hell. Yet, in our fear, we carry our own hell with us and leave the seeds for their dark deeds.

The evening was too still, for although I managed to relax enough to play with you because your exuberance was so hard to resist, we were tense to breaking in the stillness; every sound seemed to carry too far, too loud, too fast. It was as if the very air had control of us.

Obviously of a quiet nature, you didn't need to bark, expressing yourself quite adequately in many other ways, your every movement a perfect gesture, a communication so instant and spontaneous that you could not but be understood.

We had arrived on time at our meeting place, a small tangled human mass of relief and apprehension. I had driven us to this remote field only to find that Rik, our driver, was not there waiting. My stomach turned over; a sickness threatened to reach my throat. Everything had been planned; each detail put in place with the care of the experienced. To fail at this point when the most difficult part was over, would be a disaster too terrible. We clung to your freedom. Anxiety expressed itself in taut silence.

We had let you all out on to the grass in the field, one by one, discretely, quietly. We avoided each other's eyes when they darted with cautious apprehension, but they met in mutual amused approval of the pleasure as noses met grass and trees in an appreciation so immediate that only an animal or a child could feel.

And then I began to run with you, running fast away from the darkness and fear which made our hearts brittle to breaking. This was true even for the most practical among us; we were haunted.

This suffering wrecks lives.

You had to go, just for three weeks, to a place even I could not know. You would have the tattoo taken from your ear by a sympathetic vet so that you could never be claimed by them again. But I told you how it would be later when we would have all the time in the world. I told you how there would be woods and fields to run through, snow on the hills in the winter to roll in and the smell of the new mown hay for your delight in longer summer days.

You sat quite still and listened to every word as if you understood. I think you could read the pictures in my mind.

I crowded all my thoughts into our new friendship, as these precious minutes gave it space to grow into the dream of a happier future. I pushed out subversive thoughts which darted like our eyes to unwanted terrors.

We waited, suspended in time, all our perceptions and emotions growing with every breath. And in that dream our eyes met soul to soul.

I trusted that time would deliver us.

Chapter 1

Breath comes in fresh, bright gasps. Joseph is chasing Frances, laughing, and the dogs are laughing, chasing in circles, bounding at their ankles.

'You'll never catch me. My name is Free. You'll never catch me,' she laughs. 'I can fly.' The glowing green of the fields stretches to infinity.

She stops and twirls like a dervish. She does it often and doesn't become giddy easily. The dogs join the game seeking out its relevance, leaping, barking. Whirling.

'Hey, come on, time to go in,' Joe says.

'I'm not giddy yet.' Giddy: it meant possessed by a god in time long past. 'Time to go back.' It's always time to *do* something, push on.

He's insisting. She's resisting. Neither is desisting. The morning lights everything a brilliant, rose pink.

She's twisting to a pitch. *'Don't break the spell,'* she pleads *'Time.'* A relationship between moving heavenly bodies.

'We should get up early every morning and walk like this,' he says. 'Yes.' She leaps, like a child.

They've caught up with each other, side by side for a few moments. 'The children's breakfasts – back to earth,' he insists.

'Earth is a heavenly body.' She wants to embrace the whole of it. 'So are you,' he smiles.

'You are earthy,' She fends him off.

Time rules. Time flies.

'Like a never-ending stream . . . forgotten as a dream at the opening day.' She's suddenly melancholic but melancholia feeds her.

'Bears all its sons away,' he shouts, 'as will the bus for school at eight. We'll be late. I hate them to be late – then I'll have to drive them in.'

She laughs, giving in. The dogs, with panting grins, slip through the fence into the garden and Frances and Joe slip through the kissing gate with polite solemnity and one last lingering look at the sunrise which will soon be just another sweet memory and no more a soothing, roseate embrace.

The sun sends brilliance through the window, shining on the yellow walls, daffodil bright, playing, light, freed from the passing thunderclouds. A day to walk, upright and face the face of the in All.

The children have caught the bus into town. The house is quiet now they've gone. 'Frances, what now?'

Joe is irritated, uncomfortably burdened by the welling tears in his wife's eyes. It is always a stream that will not be damned, which he cannot divert. He is restless for the day, moving about the kitchen. He puts his muesli bowl into the dishwasher, moves to make more tea to take into the office. He needs to sip the strong, warm water, feel its consolation. His movements are brisk, decisive. Distant.

'How often do I have to say, don't open your mail until you've done a morning's work? Look what it does to you.'

What is it doing to him? There's a vague feeling of panic in the air. His breath comes too quickly. His rhythm is broken.

Frances is lost. She takes a deep, slow breath, opens her mouth to read a paragraph aloud but her voice is silenced by a hopeless painful tightening in her throat. She turns her head. Swallows. Defiant, the voice will out.

'Look! Look at this. I can't take any more.' *He was a man of sorrows and acquainted with grief.*

Floating on music. St Matthew's gift from God. She surrenders to self-pity and all her strength gushes away.

Frances is hunched over the long, scrubbed kitchen table. Stray cat hairs are caught up into her strangulated breaths. Grief comes to breakfast too often; she prints the invitation cards; she embraces this unwelcome guest and it consumes her, house and home. The door is never closed. She's lost the key. Maybe she was born without one? Can Joe make one?

'You'll be finished. Wrecked. For what? You are simply feeding all the wretchedness.' He picks up the offending pages. His features buckle. He places them firmly at the other end of the table. His odd perceptions surprise her.

'You've got to find detachment. How can a wreckage be constructive? It's a contradiction.' He stops. Still, now. He has closed the page of wide beagles' eyes against the page of dead primate bodies. Dead and alive.

An old, black cat with one eye jumps into the space the magazine had occupied a moment before and begins to nibble at Frances's toast, pulling it off her plate and licking off the margarine. She puts her face in its fur, her dark hair mingling with its dark fur.

'There's work to be done.' Joe is no idler. He sets his face against the morning and takes his blue and white porcelain tea cup into the office.

The film music he has written has bought them a comfortable existence. Work is his love. Application is his desire, discipline his liturgy. It braces his shoulders and pushes his chin up, with some defiance.

Frances writes scripts, but stories are a process of deep discovery for her and being human, she is uncovering wounds which she must own before she can write what she needs to.

Frances shudders. Why won't Joe make her certain she's not falling into a black hole, sure that living isn't grabbing at shadows in a pea soup fog, that not all humans are monsters?

'You're too damned practical.' A last fling at the disappearing shadow of her disappointment. He can put the shutters down at his own convenience. Sorry, closed. Frances wants to smash the shutters.

'What is it all for?' she calls out. 'What if I really could rescue them? What then?'

Joe catches the words, but doesn't parry them as he climbs the basement stairs. They would disturb him. This is the frown which layers his brow, as he shuts the office door. She knows the muscles in his back are twitching. He can fend off sticks and stones. He is armoured with muscle and intellect.

Words hurt Frances, and the spaces where she thinks they ought to be dancing, caressing, lifting, filling.

'Sometimes I think he's totally insensitive, Freddie.' She speaks to the black cat who is now licking himself contentedly. There's a trail of sticky crumbs across the table because his once broken jaw has made him a clumsy, if zestful, eater.

A bright ginger tom with cross eyes is sharpening his claws on the once substantial but now thinning table leg; a Birman cat is divesting himself of tufts of long, unwanted fur on to the cover picture of a beagle behind bars. Clumps of it are flying into a vase of yellow flowers on the brink of decay. They won't be thrown away yet; the merest hint of live colour saves them from thoughts of premature burial in the compost heap.

Frances gets up and leaves the white and yellow colours and shadow of the basement kitchen, making for her study on the first floor. Each step is an effort.

'How can thoughts become such a heavy burden?'

'Because thoughts are the stuff of things,' she answers herself out loud. Now she must enter a world where thoughts are real. The kingdom of the creative mind which greedily spreads its empire into the everyday, all borders blurred where time and space become mere empty words.

She sits at her desk; a solid oak table painted the colour of old red wine. The intensity of ancient ruby light breathes her in, comforting, strong.

She looks out on to the tree-lined gravel driveway. It has begun to rain, gently. This stream of sunlight gives a mysterious lustre to the sky, the trees, the grass, the stones and the moss, especially the moss, shining emerald green like the Irish landscape. She closes her eyes and sees a burst of brilliant purple, then yellow.

Then she opens them to the white paper before her, her words angular, jagged, in black ink. Her heart will burst.

I must know this character before I put her into an artificial frame.

She had read all about her, but she must get inside her mind. Who, Frances or Franziska, will dictate the terms?

But the pleading eyes of burnt and poisoned beagles behind bars fight to regain her attention. Is it rejection to push them away? The fountain pen is a pleasure in her hand, gold-nibbed, the ink flows smoothly making full words from a source unknown.

'September 1939.' She reads over the notes she has already written.

'A cluster of women wait shivering in the chill September dawn, guarded by three overfed SS men.' She turns back a page. Shivers. Raindrops on stone. Clouds: a million grey raindrops hiding the rainbows which a touch of sunlight might reveal. Franziska is just twenty, keen with the confidence of youth; the promise of life.

Berlin in 1934 was already a dangerous city. Franziska's mother was half-Jewish, of Hungarian extraction, her father a German Protestant Social Democrat working in agricultural research in I G Farben, a corporation permeated with Nazis. His involvement in politics has already seen him into and, by a stroke of luck, out of prison.

Frances is living on a see-saw, between the living and the dead, between animals and man, between her real family and a character upon a page, her everyday life and a dog who will not leave her mind.

She is swung to and fro almost as if she has no will, yet her will swings her on its intricately plaited rope into this maze. Something in her has cried out to see these places upon which many dare not look.

For her, it is more than her life is worth to turn away. It is like a sinister enchanted forest with clearings suffused with ethereal light.

Someone gave her Franziska and said, 'Bring her back to life' and events gave her the black dog. It would be a betrayal for which she would suffer to deny them now. She has words for them, words which may speak the silenced voice of millions, but she feels them too deeply.

These two are a crowd, an ocean of haunted weeping.

'Is this a resurrection, or am I merely walking upon graves?' 'How much love is in your heart?' sings the blackbird. 'How can I measure? I do not know myself yet.'

'Then tread very carefully and do not stay too long, stay too long, stay too long.'

Each new page is a stepping stone into her own interior – a long history dusted over with the sleep of ages past...

Joe knocks her door and steps into the room. 'I've made lunch.'

'So soon?' Us is a crowd. Frances is looking into a distance he cannot see. 'You're lost to me again.'

The words float past her. Echoes knock against one another in her head. Franziska, a doll coming alive in the hours of dark, an animated dream, more real than day.

'You've stepped out of time.' He's looking at her.

Ah yes, Joe really does have his perceptions – she is puzzled as to where they come from. His musical soul? She smiles and is pleased. He's reached her. Now he'll take her down to lunch.

'You've got to keep a distance.' He likes to produce chopped salads, French dressing, stir-fries, puff pastry, savoury scones, mushroom puddings, in his stride. His head is a full pantry, marble-lined and safe, secure.

'You don't know what it is to feel the feelings of another, to be inside their head, their heart...' 'No. But she died a long time ago.'

'What is time? What is dead?' Thoughts and feelings have no boundaries. 'Don't lose yourself.'

'I have to know. I can't stand in her light.' 'The children find it difficult.'

'I don't want to trouble them. They should be happy. Don't you make up for it, enough and more?'

There is an area of conflict. They are reaching out towards each other, but there is an inward motion which changes their direction, puts them at variance, does not allow them to see with the same eyes. He puts earning money first.

'Be practical. Just get it down on the page,' he says.

Our lives are arranged in hierarchies, priorities subordinated according to our wills, she thinks. Thoughts flash through her mind as she looks at him.

Mushroom puddings heavy with steamed flour and a ghost risen alive from the ashes of six million; the energy of vital offspring and the rotting stems of flowers decayed, the necessity of feeding the bank's ever-open throat – the impersonal greedy child of fears and desires. That's the one burden too many.

Who is in control, Joe? Mastercard, Visa, American Express?

They go to their light salad lunch. It was good of him to make it. They talk about parents' evening at school later in the week. That's easy, a safe distance from work. They put their plates in the dishwasher and pour green tea to take back to their rooms.

'Just keep borders,' he says, setting his body, sculptured ready to start the second half of his working day. He looks at her for a brief moment. She smiles. The blue of his washed denim shirt makes his eyes a brighter blue. 'The summery sky has not yet gone, despite the rain.' The thought passes swiftly through Frances's mind, there is colour, but almost unnoticed. Even when things seem dark, there is colour.

Back in her own world of the study, Frances strokes the deep red undersides of the leaves of a begonia which has grown to a giant in this room, then settles back at her desk. 'Everything passes.' She says the words aloud. This is a daily incantation. It is a ritualistic protection.

A border, a boundary. She places everything that is intolerable upon a stage – a screen is somehow too real, like visions which invade the mind unwanted, overpowering common thoughts with their wild dramas, reaching across distances suddenly become one space. But she cannot resist it. 'These are mere performances,' she says.

She becomes the audience. Franziska in celluloid.

Frances gets up, paces the room. But Franziska has been born of a real past. She is but one in this the horror spectacular with a cast of millions which did not begin in 1939. The horror had no beginning nor ending as a set-piece. The caged hatred in the heart of man did not die in 1945. Man, helpless against aeons of trapped bestiality, his goodness struggling like stray threads of sun rays on a stormy day to pierce the dull weight of darkened clouds. Before, Earth was a paradise. Before it was Eden: a vision lost millions of years ago. But is anything ever lost? All time is now. We are in all time. She loses herself in the thought.

So, too, the lost love did not die in 1939.

Frances looks through the glass at the glistening leaves. She lifts the heavy sash window and listens to the water slowly dripping. Its gentle fall soothes her drop by drop. She kneels upon the polished wooden floor and asks, as she breathes the soft damp air, for an answer, just for Franziska and then for herself. But although she dare not admit it yet, something in her knows somehow they are one and the same.

Frances will re-play Franziska in spirit before she divides her to serve what has come together in them piece by piece, a vision in pictures on a screen.

Her life too, must be divided. That is how she survives, putting life into sections. Frames of a film, night and day, life's different compartments.

This process of separation will bring some order. Frances is searching for a synthesis with which to make sense of the chaos of her emotions. It is in moments of stillness that she glimpses her purpose and she settles to make notes which fill the afternoon until the boys come crashing in later and haul her back into everyday life.

Chapter 2

Dear Dog, the world is quiet, but for the birds shrieking in the roof and making the trees a mass of song.

The sun is rising over the hills and the room is filled with a delicately pink and golden glow. The gift of a new day asks us to do our part.

Even our dogs are still asleep, undisturbed. I've taken my notebook from my secret cupboard and am undoing the tape which holds it closed between stiff covers.

I am going to write about you.

You were a free animal, living happily, judging by your faith in us, with more kindly human beings than the ones who captured and imprisoned you. Dismissing your past history as if it had never existed, they made other plans for your life, which would be paid for, and would become theirs to use as they wished: an object, a tool, a number. As soon as you got into their hands, your name disappeared and they gave you a number: B384. That is what was written on the tattoo which identified you. As an object which breathed – as they breathe – you had a use for them because even though you were denied feelings – which they reserve only for themselves – you were considered similar enough to stand the trial by their latest chemical inventions or rearrangements of older inventions which, to make more money, must continually be rearranged in order to earn the label 'new and improved', or even a new name.

Money is an artifice of man which has no connection with the natural world, the cycles of the cosmos, or the life of the soul. Those in its thrall seek power while others who learn to hate it, become embittered and alienated. It is a weapon. As a weapon in the war against Creation, it built your prison cell.

One human student of the natural world who called out in sorrow and anger at man's ravaging of the creature kingdom wrote: *It seems as if we wish to produce a human race in solitude, but in solitude that human race will have no chance of surviving.* I know all too well that the abuse of one species leads to the abuse of all others. We are joined in an eternal golden web from which we cannot escape.

What a mystery is our interconnectedness. The human mind is a trickster; it gives us false impressions of the world of which we are a part. We follow a shadow and cannot see the form. We imagine we stand alone, when we are but a small part of the myriad forms of the manifested thoughts of a Divine Intelligence, balanced so finely according to plans of such grandeur, even in their microscopic manifestations, that if we could really see this, our arrogance would be stripped to its very roots which spread so tenaciously beneath our surface: Fear. Fear, a great abyss hollowed by lack of love and Master of the Great Dark.

He reigns everywhere where we hold ourselves dear above all other life. Puppets of the shadows of our own projected thoughts, sometimes unknowingly, and in varying degrees, we seek to protect ourselves at great cost to all that lives. Unable to trust, stupefied by ingrained habitual thought patterns, we dare not look at the shadow within. Even those who begin to work for good in pity and anger are led to believe in distorted thought images which find life through fears and hatreds as yet not recognised. Seeking to put a greater house in order, we forget that our own houses still contain many dusty rooms. We are clumsy delinquents whose feet plod too heavily upon the earth, our senses numbed by desire.

Your kind smells the airy streams of life in the wind, runs lightly and demands nothing.

I have to write these things down, to try for an explanation. I owe it to you and all trapped animals to attempt an understanding.

It was September 17th that Pamela, who is a close friend, decided upon action for the 24th, rather than go along with yet another empty protest. Perhaps demonstrations really are a waste of money and energy. Their time seems to have passed. They provide occupational therapy for those in the office of our organization working to justify sizeable salaries. Am I unfair?

Pamela is practical, good at organizing, and passionate. She continues to work for nothing except the satisfaction of feeling she's playing some part in the battle for freedom. I suppose our freedom lies in rebellion against a way of life which imposes daily death sentences so numerous that except when we allow ourselves a glimpse of the truth in unguarded moments, the reality is surreal to us. A cloud of statistics, an incredible string of species: from horse to fish to fly, all born to die prematurely – floating dried and shrivelled heads, trophies in the hunt for man's immortality. When man and woman choose, the privilege of existing is simply cut, poisoned, burned, screwed, broken, crushed or crashed away.

There is a silent desperation in it. But the victims screamed.

The inquisitors smiled.

The victims scream.

And there are still smiles upon the inquisitors' faces.

Sometimes Pamela and I do not agree. Every last breath is precious for a dreamer. Pamela can see salvation in the syringe which silences the halting heartbeat when suffering reaches bounds beyond which she sees no hope.

But I see hope as eternal, stretching to the very last horizon of life; each sighing breath an empowerment straight from the Creator.

Pamela has some faith in women, while I'm unsure that sisterhood makes ties freer of human foibles. Her clipped red hair stands straight and defiant against a healthy freckled face. Her build, as sturdy as her convictions, belies a softness not allowed to escape into vulnerability. Tears would be a shock if they were ever allowed to appear, but nervousness forces an entry into that steadiness from time to time, and makes her hands shake and voice quake with emotions she would rather quell.

A meeting of the Action Group was arranged for the following Wednesday to discuss the 24th. Only a handful knew about it. The group had to be restricted in the hope that there would be no trouble, no disputes. Pamela hoped that only the six or so invited would go along because the movement had become contaminated.

There was a surfeit of ill-feeling and there were few people one could truly trust. Everyone was guilty of criticizing everyone else. Although one faction had been the most severely disruptive, I too had been a part of this pattern, but knew how destructive it was. Realizing too late that we had allowed a negative manipulative power to manifest itself through personalities who could never climb down, we had to watch them.

On the 19th we had had a meeting with the committee and staff of our organization. I came away at 9pm, long before the end. The committee had been riven in two. New ones had been co-opted, bent upon civil war. Some of our own side joined them and turned against us. Their tactics were disruptive, they constantly argued so as to wear down opposition, so that all of their resolutions would be passed when those who were opposed to their views were so weary they had no energy left to argue their corner. I was worn very thin, having alternated between pleading for reason and feeling outraged anger all evening.

I left with the sounds of their raised and squealing voices echoing in my ears. Each one had jostled for centre stage with a meagre audience but one which in their reality swelled larger. I watched as previously innocent faces took on monstrous masks, each small muscle manipulated by the ghosts of feelings eager to enjoy their freedom from the locked doors of a subconscious too long ignored.

There was a lad from Yorkshire, Wayne. He didn't cope well with complex arguments. He became stubborn and repetitive. Small and stocky, he clung to his ideas, closing his ears to any voice of dissent as if it might threaten his very existence.

Gillian, who always wore tight jeans and whose attractive face, pinched to the bone with tension which released itself in spitting bursts and hissing whiplash comments at those who dared to disagree with her, would be moved to tears and then there would be a silence. In the silence the real issue would emerge: animal prisoners in laboratories. Then there would be a momentary agreement of compassion and anguish. But then it would be submerged once more as arguments resumed.

Eventually, we were driven to find who was and who was not truly of our company. We suspected infiltrators and watched for signs, looked into the eyes of the shaven-headed newcomer in khaki clothes, checked on the antecedents of an older, balding leftover from faded protest songs, who liked to sing for freedom but never stand on the line, in case his freedom was threatened.

We watched Gillian, the office manager, flirt and smile, stamp her feet and slam the door, by turns playful, tortured, manipulating and somehow always confused. We watched veteran Marjorie's blood pressure rise, quick to feel a wrong and swoop upon administrative flaws. Older by far in years and experience than the rest of us, her impatience with what she saw as foolishness was not good for her health. Warm and always covered in dog hairs, she was mother earth in a motley family which had thrown out mothers with authority a long time before.

Elenor, a well-bred blond ex-model in her forties, who understood committees but not the indecency of others, was set adrift in a sea of the kind of faces she had never before encountered.

The law was about to change and that caused a terrible unrest. Opinions split, the offices and committees of the anti-vivisection movement were peopled by socialists, conservatives and anarchists; educated in comprehensives, a rare one from a public school, in polytechnics, in suburbia and squats, by degrees or quite unexamined, they had passed into the turmoil that was life, on the dole, doing all right or getting by. Agnostic, militantly atheist, humanist, almost Buddhist, Jewish and plain secular, they scrambled their ideas together, shifted thousands of hard-won pounds, many donated by those whose hearts willingly emptied their almost empty purses, and failed at times to keep them from the grasping hands of their opposers.

The media tempted them, made them jealous of the spotlight; knowledge tempted them – especially of the secret kind gained by investigation or by luck – tempted them to hoard and guard it; a small power whose meaning eluded them. Knowledge unshared caused yet more trouble.

Fear and defiance wrestled for control, twisting the meanings of words and making the air stale to the point of suffocation. Casualties of the infighting who departed sick or broken were instantly forgotten as so much human waste, condemned to disappear with their wounds.

Home again after a long journey from a particularly contentious meeting, I lay on the floor with the dogs for an hour, every nerve alight and burning, unable to move, unable to sleep, filled with quiet desperation. I was alone, the human family having sought the reassuring comfort of sleep. But not alone – the animals seemed to understand. Warmth and affection were about the only bearable things – words had become empty.

I seemed to be existing in an unreal world shrouded in a grey cloud which kept reason away and locked victims in with its cloying dull stickiness. It always became heavier at the office door of the organization, but followed us everywhere, colouring everyone's perceptions of everything. Even former friends seemed tainted, cloaked in its grey web. I no longer saw the world in the pure light of the sun. It stood between me and my better nature like a band of fog clouding the horizon of an otherwise inviting landscape.

Thrown into emotional confusion, several of us could not comprehend that shocking intractability of those we imagined were struggling towards the same goals.

I felt in the world as one whose mother had adamantly but mistakenly accused her of some fictitious wrong and had set her heart against her, while the truth stayed hidden in a forest of misjudgement and negative emotions enlivened by circumstances too big to change.

People judged one another by arbitrary standards, running in circles of viciousness which tugged them firm in front and stabbed them from behind.

There was an atmosphere of violence churning in those people which occasionally almost managed to erupt into physical form, but afraid to declare itself, slithered back and hid once more, behind angry words and ugly emotions.

Where will it all end?

On the 20th I could do little all day. There were many telephone calls, all concerning the current troubles. Work was completely disrupted. Each time, the adrenaline started to flow and a sense of urgency overwhelmed me. We were all saying the corruption had to be uprooted; justice had to be done. The organization had to be put back on course, but hatred and resentment seethed in the very air we breathed and any good outcome seemed impossible.

In quieter moments I longed to shut it out completely, to turn my back, walk away, but that looked like weakness, and that would open wide the gates for the experimenters to walk more freely over the animals.

Calls of 'slander', 'libel', 'assault', were being shouted. Was this all ego mania or collective madness?

Politics? Shrewd manoeuvres? Who could fathom the motivation of those who were crumbling the movement to all but dust? Was there someone there specifically placed to destroy us? But who? We threw out suggestions like juggling balls, but one by one they fell upon the floor, with barely a bounce; hollow, improbable and useless. Were we naive? Yes, but we had not seen this coming. We were punch drunk.

Small disagreements had grown into something of national interest. We consoled ourselves about the misrepresentations: 'Today's news, tomorrow's . . .' no, chips are not even wrapped in newspaper any more. But the news is never very wholesome and could never be an aid to good digestion with sensation hypes to churn the stomach into revolt. Poisonous ink.

The research professors and their entourages of compliant technicians and veterinary overseers – with their 'humanitarian' reasons for watching over the torturing of dogs and cats, must have been smiling to themselves then, nodding and shaking hands as they strutted along their small corridors of power in factory and hospital, from Porton Down to Inveresk.

And no-one heard the monkeys scream near Devil's Dyke on the genteel Sussex coast that is so healthy for retirement and no-one saw the shovelsful of dead little, oh-so-white little, rodent bodies, whose clever, intricate brains worked out too long before who was who, in their world of anguish. Too many thousands to count.

Did you and your companions feel isolated, singled out, alone? Did you have any inkling of an understanding of the dark shadows which manipulated the minds of those who imagined your life was theirs to extract? Did you feel sorrowful companionship with others of your kind? Did you, when the shadows of night's dark sent the humans away from their work, hear howls a hundred and a thousand miles away, carried across the silent air, a telepathic transfer, a communion in distress?

Did you panic in the cages, helplessly confined in an unknown destiny, a fate designed so especially by tinkering minds which had so confined themselves to their distorted focus that they had long lost sight of the whole?

Did you bite at the wire, explore your confines, touch the steel with your tongue which all too recently had caressed the hands of someone you loved, feel its sharp-smooth metallic taste grating on your soft mouth?

Or did you hope that daylight would bring a dawning in their black minds, pink as their flaccid skin, a ray of sunlight white as their coats?

Did your trust and friendliness signify hope or confusion? Or did you know something that we do not?

There is so much we do not know, Dear Dog. We could dream your freedom. And dreams can set you free.

But there were those on our own side who hated us and were condemning some of the very people who, without thought for themselves, rejected the law and went to open our cages – at least as many as they could. Perhaps they were jealous of this courage but could not name their motives. They too, were victims of their own distress.

Evil had become a reality. While occupied in petty, ruinous quarrels we were doing nothing and allowing evil to flourish.

Selfishly I could find no way out of that despair. How much worse it is for those creatures who can never sprawl on the bank beneath the yew hedge to catch the startling, fleeting warmth of thin sun rays on autumn afternoons as my cats do, content, knowing that same day will follow same day with food and love to start and round its comforting cycle. They do not know, thank God, of hands made like ours – unhappy thought – which lock and unlock steel cage doors and offer not a sign of brotherhood and sisterhood in soft caress, but harshly tug, restrain and offer only needles, screws, and poisons by the ton.

They do not know – unhappy thought – for all the times I too, might have been deaf. Those who have ears like ours but which do not hear the screams, the cries, the howls which tear at the hearts of decent men and women. Nor do they know of eyes, like ours, through which the soul can never shine: souls blackened by deeds done in the darkness of those places where a conscience does not live, nor pity flicker across a face even for brief moments' grace before it dies. The happy creatures in their safe contentment do not know, thank God, those secret places where those of our race busy themselves in monstrous undertakings and break the veins of friends. As my heart breaks, so in the gutters of humanity shall our blood together flow. They do not know of these steel-locked, neon-lit cells where Death manufactured daily, eats of itself and gnaws, unseen, unnoticed, at the diseased heart of humanity.

It is this collective guilt we all must share if we pass by, avert our eyes or let our consciences, unattended, unheeded, die within us.

That evening, I stirred all former sorrows into consciousness with too much weeping – such weakness.

Such defeat had to stop.

Chapter 3

Frances, at her writing desk, in the room in the house she so loves, reads and reflects upon the work in hand. The endless facts in history books are simply history. A scrubbed blonde whitened laboratory of a world constructed upon the charred bones of the dispensable: six, or perhaps seven million Jews, Gypsies, Jehovah's Witnesses and Social Democrats, the outlawed by belief, the handicapped and homosexual; life's resistors and protesters, those designated mongrels, impure, unfit to be part of the New World Order.

Frances holds the relic of a life which came into her possession by a curious coincidence – from a German her agent had met at a party – a dusty faded gift calling to be unwrapped, its precious secret yearning to be revealed: Franziska's secret diary. Her namesake, a lifetime away, but not apart.

The little book blossomed and withered by turns, its pages seasons of the soul, a spectre of years building to a sacrifice carried with her like a wound of honour, sorrow and glory since her entry into the storm-tossed waters of a world still at war with itself in 1917.

Frances searches every last bare and broken twig of the wintered lives and breathes full in those days which light up the spirit of Franziska's life, alive and bursting with colour, where the red and grey and black of outward events mix with the golden and purple of her inner untouchable self, raised up above the reach of her destroyers. As she reads, Franziska's life transfigures her own.

August, 1929
Mama always says the last war didn't end, that it still breathes like a monster not slain. Aunty and Papa do not reply when she speaks like an oracle but a cloud moves across their faces, making a shadow over

each line of care and experience, and their eyes wander into empty space. I shiver, Mama holds my hand and her hand is cold. I am sad because I feel as if she is not near me and I cannot hold her. Her dark green eyes are wild worlds beyond my reach. In them I see her longing and fear for me. I stroke her deep black hair; my fingers are caught in its dark curls and a smile settles around her soft generous mouth.

Papa says things to Aunty – his beloved sister – that he will not say to Mama with her visions and excitable feelings. Papa has always been involved in politics and he, too, admits he has been uneasy for the last seven years. He has a special young distant cousin, Bertholdt, who comes to see us sometimes. They shut themselves in Papa's study and talk secretly of political matters. Bertie has the most beautiful smile in the whole world. When he smiles at me his face glows and his blue eyes sparkle. When he goes away again, I cannot forget him. I hold him with me. I hold his smile. He is already a grown man of twenty and I am considered by everyone still as 'the little one'. But they do not know how I read their minds and feel their hearts and am troubled by their protection which excludes me. Bertie and Papa are socialists. They talk of how the Jews are being blamed for all of Germany's problems. Our country wants to be great, to reach its might into Africa and rule again. The Nazi party has gained seats in the Reichstag and Bertie and Papa fear that people will be helplessly attracted to their extreme and irrational attitudes.

September, 1929
Aunty's house. The sweetest smell of late mown hay and fresh picked grapes fills me full of happiness. I wish the sun would always shine as warm and bright as this and the holidays never end. I do miss Mama and Papa sometimes in the evening when the sun goes down and darkness creeps nearer but it is so good to be in the country.

I think of Papa's silky grey hair and the sad heavy look in his eyes when he talks to Bertie, who only smiles back because he is a young man, I suppose, and not so full of the anxieties which older people always seem to carry with them.

As I set off for the baker this morning, Aunty caught me by the arm. She is always so round and warm and soft and her brown hair caught the sunlight and glinted like dark polished copper. Then a sadness suddenly came into her eyes as she looked at me, and a firmness in the grip of her hand called me to attention: 'Franzi, don't speak with the Schmidt boy or the Fischer family – just *Guten Tag*. Be careful, little one. That curly dark brown hair, those eyes,' I heard her mutter to herself as she turned away. Then, 'Go on then, my beauty,' she called as she looked over her shoulder.

I wanted to laugh, and I tossed my head to feel my long thick curls bounce about my neck but a pain like a spike prickled my limbs and so I nodded and ran to fetch the bread while it was still hot from the brick oven, free as a bird and eager to catch the first warm loaves.

February, 1930

The SA killed eight Jews last month. Papa has been saying more often lately that we should not mention grandma who is safe in heaven. My beautiful mother was always so proud of her. A brave free spirit, she married a gentile but carried the poetry of the Psalms in her heart and gave her heart to her only daughter. Papa was brought up as a Protestant.

August, 1930

I was in the town with some friends today. Aunty didn't want me to go. The brown shirts chased us and one of them grabbed my arm very roughly to make me do the Hitler salute. I have a large blue bruise. They are mindless ruffians. I must hide it from Aunty or she will see more danger around every corner and tell me not to go here and there and I'll feel like a poor dog chained to its kennel.

December, 1930

The papers are full of stories of unemployed people. One hundred and seven Nazi deputies have been voted into the Reichstag. Papa was there as they marched in. We heard people shouting, 'Germany awake, death to Judah!' Papa's voice is lowered when he speaks of it, as you would speak of a person who is seriously ill and Mama nods her head a great deal and listens to him with her dark eyes wide. I watch these things, but mostly feel I am not part of them. I can feel the mountains, warm sunlight, glistening snow, purifying everything. My head is in the mountains far away from the stifling uniforms which stamp about the streets and into Papa's once-peaceful evenings.

I go into the garden and talk to the birds. Squirrels eat nuts from my hands and there is a sprightly little robin who will peck from my fingers. With them all is calm, as if nothing would ever change except Nature's seasons.

But we too have seasons and my moods change. When I am taken to the sunlit mountains – sometimes in the middle of dinner, or walking along the street or in the midst of a class in school – I know it is because somehow the Creator has something different in store for me and that is His way of holding me in the palm of His hand, just as He does the robin and all the chattering sparrows who squabble with the pigeons in the *Teirgarten* for crumbs. Now I want to cry, but from what part of me do these unwanted tears come? Is it because there is so much that seems just beyond the reach of my knowing? I stay in my own world and live as much as I can in my visions, in the beautiful places far away. It is not difficult to be in two places at once, but I tell no one about it, not even Mama or Aunty. I share the other world with others than those dear to me here in this world.

August, 1932

I have been lying in the herb garden reading Heine poems until the sun made my eyelids heavy with light and heat. My nose is full of pungent green mint, limey lemon balm and deep purple lavender which seems to clean the air with each sighing breath of the summer breeze. The bees are humming in my head. I am light as the rouge-tinted butterfly brushing lovingly against scarlet paper poppy petals, so fine that we must not touch them with our heavy human fingers – one unthinkable movement and some terrible damage might be done; sweet unearthly beauty harmed, destroyed. Nature is so utterly delicate and yet mighty beyond our meagre human abilities. The thinnest poppy petal, the finest butterfly, the smallest touch of lavender, these too have power, a power to reach some inward part that lifts us out of the place where avalanches crush, gales destroy or seas engulf us. Aunty Isabelle is calling...

The lines upon my dearest Aunty's face were drawn straight and heavy when I walked into the shaded kitchen. It was as if some stranger had been in and brushed away the morning's sunbeams and had drawn in grey across her smiles. What is the matter with her? She knows she has to tell me something not good. She had been speaking with Papa on the telephone. The Nazis have now gained 230 seats in the Reichstag. Papa and Bertie are pushing with all they know against this national socialist tide which they fear may engulf us and become a monster.

We put our arms around each other and stand still in the silence, not even listening. My family is different from those of my friends. We are always so involved – others seem to be unaware of anything happening and we do not speak about it to them. We chatter and laugh with them as if life will always be the same. In fact, although it is unspoken, it is a matter of prudence, caution. The air where people gather buzzes with something quite utterly opposite to the harmony of this summer garden. This afternoon there are whisperings in the breeze – I try to catch the voices and swear I hear my name. I shiver in the sun and fear the loss of love.

January 30th, 1933
We heard today that Herr Hitler has become chancellor. A cold wind blows through our house. No-one smiles today. Everyone shivers. Winter is all around us. Papa watched the night-time parade they put on to celebrate. It was frightening and horribly awesome. Germany is entering a dark door in its history. What lies beyond?

February 19th, 1933
Hitler has been chancellor for three weeks. Thousands of people joined a demonstration in the Lustgarten Square. Art, research and the press are all now being censored. Papa and I went to the demonstration. The SA were firing bullets in the air.

February 27th, 1933
It is very cold. There is snow, but in the evening the sky in Berlin turned red. The Reichstag has burnt down.

February 28th, 1933
An unemployed Dutchman has been arrested. They say he was at the scene of the crime and claim he did it on the orders of the KPD, the Communist Party.

Papa has heard from his contacts that they have arrested 8,000 people in Germany, with 1,500 from Berlin. There is a new Decree, 'For the Protection of the People and State,' the Reichstag Fire Decree. The headline in the *Volkische Beobachter* newspaper reads, 'Now the Clampdown Will be Ruthless!' Suddenly we have lost all our freedom. Nothing is private for us anymore. Papa believes the Nazis set the Reichstag on fire so they could do this to us.

I am afraid for Papa and Bertie because the new government is making lists of all dissenters. We are dissenters who do not agree with the Nazis and we are now in very real danger. We must be extra vigilant. They are setting up concentration camps for dissenters and we hear that judges no longer have to stay within the letter of the law. There is no protection. I am so afraid that Papi and Bertie are dancing with death.

March, 1933

The SA are allowed to run wild in their horrible brown shirts. They are breaking into peoples' homes and no one can stop them. Papi calls them, 'an ignorant mob'. They are an auxiliary police force that is crashing into our lives with no restraints.

March, 1933

The weather is now very fine. It is a beautiful spring, which seems so strange with the background of secret terror lurking in the shadows.

The day was made even better when we got a surprise visit from Bertie this morning. He was wearing dark glasses and looking very respectable indeed. He doesn't want to draw attention to himself. Our dear maid, Birgit, made us a picnic in a basket and the three of us went to the Grünwald to eat it on the grass in the sunshine.

As we sat there, a small group of young teenagers walked by on a hike. They are obviously Hitler Youth. As they passed us, they called out *Jude verrecke* like a chant. This seems to be their new greeting since the boycott of Jewish businesses led by Julius Streicher. Papa just smiled a cynical smile, Bertie turned away. I looked at Papa and admired his calm while feeling cold inside in that fine spring sunshine, but when Bertie turned back and gave me one of his beautiful smiles, the world warmed up again.

He hints that he has a network of people who think like us. We feel encouraged and yet it is such a heavy task with the whole weight of the State wanting to gag us completely. They call it 'alignment' but it is coercion. An evil spirit stalks our land and ancient Moloch will demand his sacrificial victims, of that I am sure. Perhaps that is our destiny.

March, 1934
Bertie has replied to my letter! He asked me to keep our letters just between ourselves. I hid it inside my red jumper tightly warm against the chill wind still blowing. I ran to my room to savour each sweet word like ripe fruits newly plucked, so full of juice and colour and sun. I am so warm. My heart beats so fast it takes my breath away. I close my eyes to feel it all the more. Bertie has sent me a poem by my favourite poet, Heinrich Heine, *You Are Like a Flower*.

> E'en as a lovely flower,
> So fair, so pure thou art;
> I gaze on thee, and sadness
> Comes stealing o'er my heart.
> My hands I fain had folded
> Upon thy soft brown hair,
> Praying that God may keep thee
> So lovely, pure and fair.

At first, I could not breathe and then I cried because there were tears as well as love in the lines. Was Bertie also afraid of what might come? No one talks to me really honestly of these things. No one is sure what will happen. They want the young to live in hope. Papa says Bertie burns with passion and bursts with courage, that he would give his life for his friends. Why must he say these things?

He has signed off with a tenderness which fills me with longing for his smile, a longing which becomes a pain I never want to lose.

May, 1934

Bertie warns that because I G Farben is full of Nazis, they are putting anyone with socialist ideas in the new concentration camps. Papa must be especially careful. 'Look after your dear father. I kiss you tenderly, Your Bertie.' I put this letter in my secret drawer and retie the pink ribbon which keeps the small precious pile together. Then I run to Papa in his study and throw my arms around his neck. His body is lean and fit but still soft and his eyes squint from reading for hours on end.

'What is the matter?' he asks.

'Is I G Farben full of Nazis?' I blurt out.

'Pretty much, I suppose,' he replies, surprise lifting his heavy eyebrows. 'Who told you this?'

'Oh, a friend,' I shrug . . . 'You have to be careful, Papa, having been a Social Democrat. They don't like it.'

'A man cannot change his deepest convictions any more than a leopard can change his spots, *Liebling*.' He smiles. 'But I am by no means reckless. Now young Bertholdt, he should be more careful. He's a very gifted young man, but impulsive, outspoken. His heart might sway his head and that would be a tragedy not just for us, but for many, many more.'

My head becomes light and spins with these words. I knew in my heart that Bertie was doing something important. I do not ask Papa any more.

June, 1934

Papa has been arrested. His cell is on the way to school. He is locked away in the basement of the police station. I want to shake the gates and shout every time I pass it by, but silence is the only wise course. We have to wait and see. I pray for him morning, night and every spare minute of the day. Mama is surprisingly calm.

Last night I heard Mama sobbing, but I didn't dare go to her.

July, 1934
Great rejoicing! Papa is home again. As God's great good fortune would have it the man with the keys to the gate and to the cells was in the artillery in the First World War with my dearest father, so he just let him out, let him walk free! He looks surprisingly well, but he seems to limp more heavily on the leg which broke so badly in the war. The injury which may have saved his life so often gives him pain. Sometimes when he winces and his hand goes to his knee, I feel a sharp needle darting through my own leg and I turn away. What is there to do? Together this evening, we sat close and I rested my hand upon that knee, in silence.

Mama's smile is radiant and she has been crying with joy. Her eyes are shining. If Bertie were here now our happiness would be complete.

July, 1934
Several platoons of brown shirt Nazis waving a flag passed me as I was walking home today. I refused to salute.

'If you don't salute next time, we'll have you,' they shouted, but I didn't look and hoped they hadn't seen me shaking as they laughed together at their threats.

I am writing to Bertie that I want to help him fight the Nazis instead of going to college in the autumn. I mailed the letter with fear and trembling because I haven't heard from him in weeks and weeks and the family are still unaware of our correspondence. (I nearly always manage to collect the mail from the box by the gate. I made it my chore and so I have the key).

I ran home from the post office only to find the drawing room shrouded in despair as if there were to be a funeral tomorrow.

'What is it?' I felt clumsy being hot, red-cheeked and out of breath in this still, solemn atmosphere.

Mama, who had obviously been playing the piano before the news arrived, had a white lace handkerchief over her mouth, so white against her flowing dark emerald dress. The sunlight was catching a ruby ringed by diamonds on her clenched hand. Smooth skin, tinged the lightest, beautiful olive, long fingers.

Papa stood square, his shoulders back, a soothing white and pink hand on her shoulder. He stretched the other towards me, beckoning, with his fingers, not longer than his palms, hands that grasp matters, a comfort. I moved towards this strong, sure, sensitive hand.

'Bertie, my love.' He said it so gently, I flushed even more crimson – did he know? Then I panicked . . . 'Yes, yes?' I asked. But something inside insisted it could not be the worst.

Papa hesitated.

'He was so handsome, a beautiful young man,' Mama choked, so calm and dignified in her hurt. Filled with dread, I looked at Papi.

'He was arrested. Badly beaten up. Damaged.'

We all put our arms around each other and squeezed tightly for comfort.

Praying that God may keep thee
So lovely, pure and fair.
So lovely, pure and fair.

Bertie. I do not want to imagine what has happened to his beauty – I see only the Gestapo, their ugly sneering faces and I make a silent solemn promise to the Creator that I will stand so long as He shall let me live, with love and truth and pity. I will not run away from the bully, the tyrant, the traitor in our midst who sours the hearts of our countrymen and women. Because of this, I did not weep. My mother is lost in emotion, but I see in Papa's face that he is a little surprised at my composure. I am sometimes afraid for Mama, when she seems like a flower whose stalk will snap in the storm. I feel something like a core of steel inside me which will resist come what may. Sometimes I wish it would let me go. But it will not. I have to remain responsible, vigilant – for something. For them and something more, for Bertie too.

Chapter 4

Frances gets up from her writing table and wanders outside, to feel the air in her face, to rid herself of clinging doubts, to feel grass beneath her feet, the earth, the earth. There is always a welcome from the earth, but the dog draws her back. She goes to write again, not of Franziska as she should, but of what is pulling at her mind.

Dear Dog, I search you out and wonder how you are coping with that strange place. Time passes. Light comes after dark. I promise you freshness in the autumn air, full with the rich smells of fallen leaves not yet rotten, but rich with their own promise; a soft bed to lie on, and dying to their colours, food for the earth on which they fall. Dead branches broken by the wind, cracked, snapped easily in the hand to half an arm's length and thrown through the air for your pleasure. Leaves for cats to leap at, fluttered in windy gusts, nailed by claws; a tame prey but a pretty one. And when the leaves are left skeletal veins, dried out or heaped, damp, mushed into a mass no longer of separate parts, you will be leaping for the love of life, a personality apart, strong-veined and cleansed by country air.

On the 22nd six of us were going to look at the laboratory we intended to raid. I told no one at home, but planned to tell my husband before I left. I didn't want him to put any doubts or questions in my mind, for impulse and instinct had become one in our decision. Despite his receding hair line, which made Joe look reassuringly older that he was, I was wilful enough not to want to trust his opinion of my actions. I no longer wanted a father-figure, only a friend I could rely on. Finally, I told him I was going to meet a friend.

The other five were wholly to be trusted. The laboratory was not so far from our home – fifteen miles or so. We lived almost in its shadow. A friend told me that she had always experienced a feeling of being utterly drained when she was in its vicinity. This happened before she knew that experimental animals were kept in this place. The same feeling casts its shadow whenever she passes other, similar places. These observations were a surprising revelation from someone so practical. Perhaps she is sensing the fear and a part of her reaches out and resonates with the fearful ones.

We met at the pre-arranged spot outside the town and were able to look around undisturbed. There was just one house opposite the building, standing across the road, but all of its lights were out and there was no sign of life. The actual laboratory buildings were relatively unprotected and could easily be reached via the yard of an adjacent jam factory. Trucks were always parked there and there would be no one working on a Saturday. The fence between the yard and the Biotox building was merely a piece of wire – some barbed, but easily cut, and not too high. Their security system, unlike many others, appeared to be basic. We heard howling coming from some prefabricated sheds.

I think that was what changed Pamela's mind.

She decided to come back with me and stay for the night, but said nothing to the others. When we arrived home, she said that we should try and get some animals out. It looked so easy, why miss the opportunity? We could both still hear the howling inside our heads, but said nothing. Practicality is paramount. We decided that it should be done the following night, as the cover of the demonstration no longer seemed necessary, and the sooner it was done the better. Rik would be told the next morning, but not over the telephone.

Pamela went to bed, but unable to sleep, I went over and over the planned rescue in my mind, trying to clear a lucid path to the dawn, swallowing fearful thoughts, wondering.

Frances looked at the stars which so many animals may never see ... and hoped for the sun tomorrow.

She slept restlessly, her dreams were mixed and disturbed, but woke feeling hopeful, if tired. The sun was shining and the day was warm and still. She took the dogs for a short walk and the world seemed so still that she felt it was waiting; it was as if the earth was standing ready. She wanted to be in the midst of that stillness, and dissolving, be a part of the stopping of time, all things held. No gravity.

Rest.

A longing for that oneness – the stillness was real and yet it remained a longing, but also was only a hope.

With that thought the heart quickened, the dogs leapt up at her, strangers came walking along the path.

The world drowned out the sound of the grass growing and she had to return.

She had to put the laundry into the washing machine, water the plants, ask the children to tidy their rooms, sort through the post, ring the plumber and fight off a rising anxiety with too many pieces of toast.

She talked with Pamela for too long, sifted through facts, mixed fact with opinion, shaded truth with feelings and came to a point where only one thing was important, that nothing should spoil the rescue operation.

They met the others at eight o'clock as planned. No one was late. One or two were early. They told them about the decision – the response was one of relief rather than surprise or objection. After discussing detailed instructions, they drove to Biotox. Pamela had told Rik to meet them with his van half a mile away at Forestry land where it would not be unusual to walk dogs, at a spot where a strong growth of trees gave good cover. They could transfer the animals to him and he would take them to a secret holding place, a safe-house, for three weeks so that they couldn't be traced.

They would then be re-homed. Frances had already decided to keep one dog herself.

She used her own car, the number plate altered. Every minute was accounted for. Deviation could mean lives.

Four were to go in, one was to remain as lookout; she was to stay, ignition key at the ready.

The engine of her car is quiet, but it seemed to roar with unaccustomed fury in the stillness of the evening.

The place was deserted. She parked inconspicuously in the entrance to a lane, by an opening to a field two hundred yards away from the building. They would be able to leave alongside the yard of the jam factory and walk along behind the cover of the hedgerow. Everyone's nerves were stretched almost to breaking.

No breeze stirred the meadow grass or the trees heavy with leaf clumped in a corner of the field. The curtains to the front room of the house opposite Biotox were drawn; the family were almost certainly installed in front of the flickering screen, glued, she hoped, for the evening, to whatever filled their lives and replaced their imaginations, or filled the vacuum where long-dead consciences once flickered tentatively, like the pictures on the box, so easily switched off.

Anger at their apparent complaisance rose in her. To condone is to take part. Spikes in her mind. Beginning to shake, she vented silent righteous anger on the faceless family who stood for all the uncaring blank faces who walked free and whose freedom seemed as useful as a volume of Shakespeare to a starving illiterate.

Living death.

And living death across the road.

Time and time again looking at crowds of empty, unlovely faces she asked – that they should die for this? A part of her was dying in her anger, for weren't those half-dead suffering too? It is the suffering of a deprivation so ageless and terrible; it cannot be named.

Anger bubbling quietly, dangerously, taking too much attention. To listen, look, be aware was all important. Be ready. Anger replaced fear. Waiting. The minutes were too long. The second hand slowed by anxiety did not lose its steadiness as did her pulse.

Looking back along the road: a car approaching – chequered stripes on its sides? Something on top? A police vehicle. . . Gripping tightly, knuckles white. Don't move. No sound, fast approaching. She stops breathing, hears her heartbeat.

It passes. Doesn't stop. 'Ken's Kabs' blazoned on its sides. Stupid. Oh stupid imagination. Thank you. She says it aloud to an unknown protector. Softly. Twice. No, three times. Three is a lucky number. Stick at three. Don't say it again. Stop those neurotic, chaotic thoughts. So foolish. Uncontrolled. Fighting me. What if? Stop them. But if? No, do not imagine anything. Suspend thought. Listen. Watch and wait. That is all you are required to do. And it is not very much. A cyclist. His light wobbling. Damn. That is all we need, some curious local. Don't let them come till he's past. Perhaps he'd be sympathetic? The sympathizers are growing in number every day. But people do not often react well on the spur of the moment, unless already inwardly prepared. Strange emotions rise up in them, emotions which were not really strange, but living quietly hidden behind the everyday face of sleep. Is he cycling mechanically? Pedalling along without seeing the world? Or is he curious? He could remember the car. Anything.

She did disguise a number on the plate.

Pedal faster. Get away. He's coming past. Don't look. She slips down in her seat. She wills energy into his cyclist's calf and thigh muscles and hopes that they are not beef-fed. But maybe, mother moon, now casting her bright silver silence about us is protecting this small mission? She knows that a moonlit night is not a good time for escape. She thinks of Franziska – on every moonlit night.

An owl swoops in front of the windscreen. She shivers, but does not know why, for she loves the sound and sight of owls, round-eyed, still and blinking.

A bark. Another. They're coming. They mustn't make too much noise. Have the tele-viewers got their box turned loud? Their blunted sensitivities; the louder they turn it up, the deafer they'll become, as their heads fill slowly with the froth, the holes taking over the brain, bubble by bubble, solidifying into gawping old-age. This is pure anger. It bubbles in her. Furiously.

Here they come. Five figures almost indistinguishable one from the other in their black acrylic balaclavas. Their pace quickens. She wants to get out, run to them, but that is not the plan. She sits tight. Every muscle taut. Wait. Anxiety gradually giving way to relief. Five dogs. Five. No panic. Calmness keeps the dogs calm. Everybody in. Close the doors quietly. No slamming. Two in the back space, two on laps in the back seat. One beside me on Pamela's lap. Black, brown-eyed, soft, tail wagging. I glance briefly, but do not wait to start the engine. There was no mud. Thank God, it hadn't rained. The car should move easily out of the hardened tractor ruts. She starts the car, but it stalls. Damn. The service light is showing. Why didn't they get it to the garage last week? She tries again.

'You should've brought Joe's car,' Pamela says, edgy.

'He would have hit the roof,' Frances says. 'He doesn't know what I'm doing tonight.'

'Please God, start this car,' she whispers under her breath. It jolts, then starts, kangaroo-style, but then they are on their way. Sighs of relief.

After a quarter of a mile, someone speaks. Safe. Confidence grows. The car is an estate; bright and silver shiny; quite new and respectable; unlikely to be stopped. Stripped of stickers; cleaned of commitment, blending blandly. Blessed, she allows herself to breathe more deeply.

'That was an easy one,' Pamela was grinning. Her newly undressed head of hair stood ruffled and on end.

'I wish we could have taken more,' Shirley sighs, lighting one of her roll-ups for the relief of it. Streetwise from suffering, her heart had grown big from a lifetime's deprivation. A universal mother, she could weep and swear with equal ease, but never on raids. She rose to every demanding occasion with a humour which never failed to surprise anyone, if only because of the circumstances in which it always surfaced. 'These are all stolen – two collies, a black lab mix, a terrier, a mongrel. How bloody dare they?'

Descriptions of those left behind began to sting the eyes; the regret tempered only by the presence of the five in the car, confused, remarkably quiet, one whining. Janet, a tiny mousey girl who only ever seemed to speak in sharp whispers, was quick to offer comfort. She always seemed strangely unmoved by the world, but shaken to the heart by the sufferings of animals, as if they tapped some great grief hidden deep in her soul.

'The smell of the place, bloody stinking.' Shirley usually swore, but the hard words always ring softer for her good humour.

Gloria the tall peroxide blonde, statuesque and in her forties, was Irish by ancestry but had spent years with her lover in a damp flat in Bermondsey crowded with animals. Rescuing animals and protesting loudly in their defence was what pleased her most.

Barbara was not long out of a smart school. Pink streaks in her spiked hair and her tight patched jeans spoke for the wild and rebellious part of her; a strike against her military father and her mother's passive acceptance of the rules and the etiquette of the officers' mess. She wanted to clean up the world and purge her soul of the sins of her father. A dedicated hunt saboteur at weekends, she would soon go to university and continue to raise hell – and endeavour to vanquish it.

They were a mixed group bound only by an uncompromising conviction.

That stuffy, strange threatening smell hung in the car. Does it hang on the experimental scientist as he goes home? Does he bathe, perfuming, soaping his clogged pores with the products he has tested before touching his wife? Or does he communicate those smells, does he impart his stickiness? Does she, crimson-nailed and scarlet-lipped, symbolically comply with this savage view of nature in which they conspire to grant man an eternally lustful role?

There is no fear now. Only anger still, and love; a lot of love layered over with anxiety for the dogs. They drive, two miles, two and a half. She counts the tenths on the mileage clock, each one a step nearer safety. There is laughter in the back. Nervous, venting laughter. They managed the whole operation so neatly. The security system had not been too difficult to handle. The place had not been touched before, so the company unusually uninfected by paranoia, had not installed elaborate security precautions – not that even those proved too formidable for the more experienced, and there are always consultants to be found. Determination and careful planning had beaten many an impact-resistant door and circumvented new and improved complex alarm systems. A few basic tools – wire cutters, a screwdriver and a basic knowledge of electrical circuitry, had served their purpose, but the lock had opened easily. The fence had given way to the wire cutters without resistance, as had the hidden electrical deterrents; no unfeeling electric eyes were left to betray them. With detailed planning and a few more participants, the way would have been clear for more animals to have been taken, but in the circumstances, neither had been possible. This small batch was a consolation for the months of bickering misery they had all endured.

The five miles passed quickly when chatter displaced counting space. Barbara even managed to joke; her spiked hair squashed to straw by the balaclava now stuffed into her pocket. We approached the rendezvous. It was ten pm.

The place was deserted. Rik's blue Ford van was not there. They fell silent and tensed for danger.

Pamela was the first to make a reassuring remark, tinged with her usual wit. Humour rarely deserted her except when engaged by red-ragged opposition. Even then it could cut quick and clean. Taking one dog each, some of them cowering, uncertain, they offered a run on the grass in the moonlight. Their excitement was intoxicating. It was easy to see that the black mongrel could be trusted off the lead. He claimed Frances then. It was as if they had long been friends. She gave him a treat from her pocket.

They had to wait, give harmless, unforeseen eventualities a chance to work themselves through.

Dancing on a knife-edge between faith and fear, she proceeded with faith.

Automatically, it danced her as the Black Dog pulled the strings.

About fifteen minutes later the sound of an engine broke into this silence of emotions withheld. The blue van.

Calm and quietly smiling, the small familiar crumpled figure in scruffy clothes and baseball cap was a warming sight.

'I thought I was being followed,' he shrugged, taking off his small round-lensed glasses to clean them, 'so I had to make a detour. But I wasn't. Sorry for the delay.'

He was stroking two of the dogs.

'Better not waste any more time.' His voice was quiet. Normal, steady.

He needed to be well away before the pubs closed when cars were more likely to be stopped. Frances wanted to change the plan. But no risks could be taken.

She had promised the dog everything, she ran her finger along the groove of his forehead, down his black nose as they said goodbye until three weeks on, but she knew he would be back and she would be waiting.

She remembered a puzzled look in his eyes, but she looked at all of them, touched each one, then patted the black one gently and he wagged his tail.

Then the van doors were closed and she stood watching him disappear, being driven off to a place of safety. Common sense had taken feelings by the hand but an uncommon sense fought for precedence.

She could not reach through his confusion. We both had to run for safety with our silent tears.

She was home by eleven fifteen. Presumably the theft of the dogs would be discovered? A feeder would go in in the morning. They would soon find out.

She fell on to the large sofa in the drawing room and talked incessantly for two hours to Joe – a release of tension, her remarks repetitions, the plans uncertain. He listened, sometimes distracted by odd things which took his attention and she complained, demanding attention as she only half-noticed the marks on the cuffs of his shirt-sleeves and the mud stains on his new putty-cream cord jeans. He had obviously been gardening in them. Everyday details had become unimportant, almost non-existent. Things which once would have caught her eye – for she constantly wanted to order chaos – faded from sight. A more vivid reality had taken over. Joe was upset she hadn't told him the truth – even somewhat angry, calling her reckless.

The black dog's card would almost certainly have been used the following week for the testing of some new drug or poisonous product.

He had been labelled, possibly by a woman. Someone who surely could not have looked into his eyes. If only perhaps, because their own were dead. He would have had to watch them, moving about, automation-like, designing his death.

These were family men and women who lived with children and pets, in homes which appeared to be just like other peoples'. They had conveniently split their lives into compartments; divided their emotions, cut themselves into neat parts, imagining that one would not, could not, impose upon the other. They would be lauded doctors and professors, technicians with florid and sallow faces; with dead blue eyes and dull black eyes: some hide behind spectacles, but others blatantly look out, until, that is, someone silently names them. Then a kind of flailing fear appears, or even a stark terror curious to behold. It is not easy to probe the most accomplished practitioners of this black art for, long ago, feelings failed them and the intellect, untempered, held sway, cold and strong as steel.

Only the purest love dare reach toward that place. Pure and unconditional. The animals have this. She saw something of it in the black dog's eyes: a deep, almost incomprehensible forgiveness.

Did he see in us the difference? Surely yes? Or did he trust all human beings? Surely, he saw life in us, not death, which shadows them as surely as this night will work its course across the face of the earth?

Did he feel puzzled, confused, afraid or betrayed that he'd left the welcoming arms of a friend so soon?

He is in safe hands. He will be warm, fed, watered, petted. No fear.

Are my thoughts reaching you, she asks herself? She wonders now. I can see you so clearly. We shall have great times together, times to cancel all the bad memories of those people in white coats with dead eyes. No fear, black dog, their images shall be expunged from the reflecting depths of your shining eyes by our radiant happiness.

Frances woke the following morning with a feeling of unease. Why? It was a day of dancing light, soft clouds and fluttering leaves, and the family were cheerful. No adolescent moods. She was brought China tea to sip in bed, and as they looked out over the hills, the sun was caught in a patch of golden-red earth across in the valley. Birds were singing, scuttling and shuffling under the eaves. Nature proclaimed her abundance from every corner. She could not define the feeling. It clung to her. It was as if something, somewhere, was wrong and she could not wash it away, shake it off. Her mind darted around the clashing personalities who had engaged them in the months of battle before she'd pleaded with it to stop. Look for the good in everyone.

Look for something good. Underneath, they all care about the animals we want to save. She is lost in thought.

Euphoria had claimed us the previous night. Was this the price of our indulgence? Why does she imagine there is always a price for emotion? She dreaded the demonstration; human beings collected together in a mass generate such mixed and jagged atmospheres. The aggression sometimes propagated on these occasions drains the psyche. Perhaps others do not find this so. Would there be any point, or would we, once more, be shouting to the wind without even one straw to clutch at?

At ten twenty, the telephone rang and forced her from her reverie. It was Pamela. The police had been to her house to make enquiries about information they had received concerning a proposed raid. Was she the organizer of the group? She said nothing more on the telephone. She said she would come over and would be arriving in about an hour.

The unease welled up in Frances's throat. She began to shake a little, but said nothing to the others about this anxiety. Suddenly indignation appeared – someone must have spoken out of place. Someone had deliberately slipped in a word where silence was the only right course.

Pamela blamed the two who came to the meeting. Caught up in a flurry of outrage, she too, accused.

The indignation could not be contained. She would accuse them face to face.

But no, because of the dogs, they had to be silent. For their sake, they knew they must not speak.

We all need to learn the value of not speaking, just as she knew

Franziska had had to learn. The value of right thought; the value of the quiet and gentle overcoming the loud and the tough.

Through aeons, water wears away stones. But unable to watch the process, we tend to discount the result.

Patience is hard to imagine, let alone incorporate in our minds. Perhaps we too, want to shout too much?

Shout 'me!' instead of listening.

At midday, strangely, the police had said nothing about the dogs. Had their loss not been discovered? Pamela said she wouldn't be surprised if the feeder hadn't bothered to go in that morning. To them, it is just another job.

As to the tip-off, Pamela was certain that our two uninvited guests, Pinkie and Sasha, actually dropped some hint to the police – out of spite? We knew that Pinkie, at least, harboured an irrational grudge against Pamela. She had seen it sometimes in her eyes, but couldn't fathom why. Luckily, however, they knew no details of the important plans.

Of course, we decided to do nothing that day, but join the demonstration and observe, if only to show that everything was normal. Rik would not be there in any case. For him, demonstrations are a futile exercise, which in a hundred years have achieved less than nothing. We would stand on the side-lines and watch...

That evening she was exhausted. There were many more police than they had expected. As they marched from the town to the laboratory, they lined the route, but when they arrived, they saw them – a menacing dark blue swarm. Oppressive, stifling, they stood row upon row, a dark blue cloud which smothered all hopes and lowered risen spirits. The marchers fell deadly silent at the first sight of them. Shocked. Hit by the hopelessness of the situation. Then suddenly, some of the younger ones came to, lashed out, fought, scrabbled, shouted, stormed the wire, ran. Their frustration rose like flame through their spines and dizzy, fire-headed, they leapt unthinking upon the backs of authority, calling out their anger. They named the forces which opposed their compassion with words from the shadows of their souls. Dregs slung like mud in coarse red heavy-helmeted faces, who iron-faced and single-minded, enforced the law which keeps the secret of the lost victims locked away. In the line of duty.

There were arrests of course. Perhaps some had come only for sensation, just a handful. Twenty or so were dragged away, arms pulled as if they would bend like rubber, not break or tear. They took Steve, Pinkie's husband, because he was one of the organizers. Frances saw blood pouring down a young woman's face as the police dragged her away, and she was shouting for her friend to take care of her child. No dissenters allowed; resisters must be silenced.

Perhaps the animals inside the buildings were frightened by the noise, especially the monkeys, but it would probably not have erupted, had the police presence not been so overbearing; a negative chain reaction. They were upholding the law; just doing their job.

Why are the creatures made to suffer for our wrongdoing? What kind of a universe allows the suffering to grow, cancer-like, unchecked?

Surely there will be nothing but death at the end of it?

Chapter 5

August, 1934
Bertie came! I have been staying with *Tante* Belle as always in the holiday, but Papa brought him out to the country to see us. Aunty was so good – she is always so motherly, so practical. She flung her arms around him and greeted him just as before, as if he looked as he always did, which he didn't. This gave me a few moments to adjust. I swallowed back the tears. I commanded my eyes to stay dry but they stung badly. And my throat ached as if I would never swallow again.

First, he hugged me, just as he hugged the others and I felt secure in his warmth. This was Bertie, not his damaged face. This soul, this immortal spirit living in a body in a dangerous place. I saw it then, all in a moment. It was as if the beautiful cloak had been ripped to rags, but beneath were still the rainbow robes. That's how I saw it, there in Aunty's garden, with the afternoon sun pouring through the leaves of the great old apple tree.

Bertie sat beside me and squeezed my hand beneath the marble-topped table, the stone still so cold in all this sun, and Bertie's hand so warm and something inside me trembled that such a contrast could be.

It was Aunty and Papa who sat opposite and had to look into his one blue eye and distract their thoughts from the livid scar down his face to keep their own faces from crumbling as they spoke – so normally – at his brokenness.

We munched our way through one of her huge fruit sponge flans and drank the big pot of iced tea and joked and laughed and we told Bertie all about the new play in which Mama was playing in Berlin and how the critics loved her and only once or twice did anyone refer to the ever-growing monster in our midst, then only to pour scorn with our laughter upon their oafish ways. Aunty thanked God Mama was so well-known and so clever. Bertie, who knew so much and could quote the poets by heart, must be an especial thorn in their boorish flesh. The breeze whispered as it rustled the leaves of the apple tree and brought the scent of roses to the table, in the full silences between bursts of conversation. In those silences, eyes would look downwards as if in sorrow or reverence, for truth and roses both have thorns.

Evening was approaching when I suggested to show Bertie my contribution to the vegetable garden. Aunty and Papa went inside to see about the preparation of supper and no doubt to work through their carefully hidden shock and pity together. They scurried into the house as the sun became cooler in its inevitable descent to the hills of the West, but no chill reached through my cotton frock that was the colour of buttery cream. I was warm as any fiery glow. I wanted to preserve these precious moments – for something unspoken threatened us yet it seemed far away – while the sun was perhaps telling me something different. We walked slowly, silently, to the vegetable garden, a sheltered spot, shielded by trees from the house and by a strong thick hedge from passing eyes. Here there were butterflies hovering among the tiny flowers and heavy scents of rosemary and thyme and lavender. Bertie kissed me for the very first time. The world was lost as my body melted into the herbs with the fading sunlight. I could smell Bertie and rosemary and felt the butterflies, and could not wait for more than a moment as I wanted to give my life away. I knew for certain then that we were woven together in some ancient web which would hold us fast together against the enemy who thought to crush all ideals of gentleness in its rush for some false glory for our land.

Bertholdt Schiller and Franziska Fröhlich were at one with the land, the earth, the plants, the birds, the sky lying over the whole of the whirling world and not separate from any living thing. We breathed with the earth and spoke silently the language of the soul and all the words and names of politics were so much dust scattered in the breeze, carried away on the wings of the infinite.

The lingering perfumes of the garden were our gateway to another place – a common inheritance: a paradise garden sunk deep in memory, yearning to be remembered and revived.

In that moment we entered it – and alas, returned. In that moment we flew above the world with its burden of suffering and yet we carried the world with us. I like to think that that moment born of our souls' momentary return brought back some small bright star to shine in our darkening land.

It was evening then and our fluttering hearts held some unspeakable knowledge that we may be entering the darkest of nights peopled by the marauding ghosts of ancient sin, that would take hold of the darkest fears of the people and make them their own. They had already shown their hand. Bertie was living evidence of that which most were unwilling to see. Even I could give it no shape, no form. Hadn't I brushed off my aunt's warnings like troublesome fluff on my coat?

Trouble and terror might come, but I could only think again and again how terrible for those through whom it will come. When the fearful bully strikes, it is the mocked and the maimed who are the victors. Bertie was here to prove it, his strong sinewy hand holding mine, his eye star-bright to the fading of the light.

When we reached the kitchen, my Aunt, so softly sure and abundant in her summer cotton flower print curves, looked up and out of nowhere exclaimed, 'For the love of God, my children, you are all lit up' and then she turned to give instructions to the maid as if nothing had happened and father came through with a glass of cold wine for everyone, smiling absently as though he were safely resigned but shadowed by sadness. There are some who know the light will come again but that they will not live to see it.

I rushed and took Papa's arm and said, 'Let's play a tune on the piano before dinner. Bertie's in fine voice.' We played and sang as if we had to drown a thunderbolt.

Mama telephoned from the theatre. She sounded very happy. The candlelight danced on the table. Aunty looked young and content in the moment. The sweet, new potatoes melted in our mouths and Bertie touched my knee beneath the snowy white lace of the tablecloth. I thought we were in a magical enchanted circle that could never be broken and I lapsed into a world whose horizon was infinity and wanted to be there for ever and ever.

'Love can never be broken,' I suddenly heard Aunty saying. The veins were showing on the back of her hand as she sipped coffee from the paper-thin white china cup. The candlelight caught on the large topaz she wore on her right hand – her only concession to glamour. 'Not the soppy stuff the crooners put about. That's all nonsense. I mean the real thing. It's beyond life and death as we know those things. To know something of it is more precious than all the treasure in the world. It is the life-giving essence, my children.' (Her fiancé had died in the Kaiser's army in 1918). She would not look at anyone as she spoke – just his photograph on the wall. She spoke with a wistful conviction into her cup. 'Yes, my children, and Papa has a long drive back tonight.'

How she still called Bertie a child, this man who had looked death in the face and came away with its marks upon his own, as if she might yet protect him with the love of a mother, from hell itself.

Tears filled my eyes as we waved them goodbye in the darkness. I was afraid for Bertie to go back to the dangers of his work, heightened now. 'Love leaves no room for fear my dear child,' said Aunty as she put her arm around me and turned us back towards the house. I knew then that she knew what was between us, for her face was full as she said the words, her eyes strong and deep with the sympathy of understanding, but held barely still upon the brink of tears. She paused for a moment, after speaking those few words and the wisdom of her silence filled the night air.

There is nothing so beautiful as the hands stretched out to reach us when we had imagined we were so alone.

September, 1934
Berlin. The holiday is ended. The country is once more a memory. I am shut up in school again and the streets of Berlin are tinged with the yellow and gold of September. The leaves, brown now, begin to fall and are trodden underfoot as the brown shirts march about in the streets: the SA – the storm section – young workers who see this uniform as an opportunity for work. They are a motley herd, incapable of questioning the motives of their drover, empty, instinctual. They seemed to be everywhere, around every corner. But now Hitler has killed their leader, Roehm, it will be the SS, who prefer black to brown. Black, the dark; they will surely be worse.

'Next time we'll get you if you don't salute. . .' Sometimes I fear we shall all fall like these leaves, victim of this storm, thrown to the ground to be trampled underfoot. All of them are victims of their own base instincts. The leaves must fall. The leaves must fall. Winter comes. Mama, Papa, Bertie, we shall need large coats against the fury of this storm.

School is changed. We choose our friends, our words, our confidantes as we would carefully choose fungi to pick in the forest – some will feed us a gourmet dish, some will make us sick, while others, should we mistake their colouring, would be the death of us.

Is it good fortune or twisted fate that I come from a family so involved, so that I find myself measuring every little change like a watchful wild animal, eyes darting, jumping at every new word which rings a note from the right?

There is a heavy storm cloud hanging in my own sky this term:

Fräulein Niemeier, our history teacher. I used to think she taught us well, but the new climate seems to be feeding some previously buried monster in her. Has she read the Nazi manifesto? Papa saw it already twelve years ago – the first edition. I was sitting on his good knee, the one which didn't hurt; he shook his head and complained bitterly to himself as the madness shouted from the pages. He could see it all, even then.

I hear him talking to Mama of inflation, of people at their wits' end, of this ghastly little man who is our chancellor, of tramps and unemployed arrested and interned. Herr Hitler's horrible promises appeal to the many who do not think for themselves but are looking for a saviour. People have a frightening hollow place in their hearts that they imagine a politician like this can save them from. I feel sure they are looking for deliverance from an empty vessel – one which will absorb all their terror, pain and grievance and anger and spew it back to them gathered up, bloated and full of angry fire. But they are blinded. Already we are seeing the results of his speeches. Some ladies seem to have fallen in love with him. Some people's faces become ugly, like Fräulein Niemeier's, as they drink in his poisoned words. Papa says if the country allows itself to be taken in by him, it will find itself ruled by fear and consumed by fire.

October, 1934
I overheard Mama and Papa talking last night. They didn't hear me as I crept past into the kitchen for a drink to help me sleep which would not come even though I longed for it. Too many threatening faces crowded in on me, among them Fräulein Niemeier's dark ringed eyes and a voice loud with the false confidence of anger set free. What dark shadow stalks her dreams to bring such dread to fuel her heated diatribes? I have told my parents nothing of the incident. The fury of a devil burned in her eyes as she smacked her large hand across my face

for daring to disagree with her vicious dogma. Now she has marked me personally with her hate.

I shivered as I crept behind the door which stood ajar. It was very late. Mama had arrived home from the theatre looking flushed, her every movement restless, her hand often raised to her bare forehead. She had brushed aside my enquiries with broad smiles which disappeared too soon. She had seemed relieved to kiss me goodnight. They were waiting to talk. I am seventeen, but they are still trying to keep me wrapped in cotton wool. When I tell Papa about what is happening at school, he looks sad, as if he might weep. There is something in his blue eyes...

I crept like a mouse – I'm light on my feet from so many ballet lessons. I avoided every creaking board – I know each little spot, I'm so used to Papa working late and trying not to disturb him with the slightest noise.

'There can be nothing in the theatre for me now, Pauli,' came Mama's voice heavy with loss.

'You'll leave as soon as we can arrange it. You and Franzi – England, you have friends there. They'll help you.'

Then silence.

'Poor, poor Fuchs.' Father was shaking his head, slowly. 'It is not so unusual now, this kind of disappearance. There are so few who can see what they will do, let alone want to stop them – until, until maybe when the terror arrives upon their own doorsteps.'

Mother listened in silence. I struggled to see through the crack near the door hinge. Her back was straight, but her head was lowered. The firelight flickered, catching the lines of concern drawn across their faces.

'Hans Fuchs was such a good writer and director – just disappeared. Vanished. Can you believe it? I can't. I can't just run away and leave you here, my darling.'

'You can and you must, my dearest.' His hand was resting on hers, reassuring, unwavering as always. 'It is by no means safe for you to stay. We knew already last year that the time would come.'

'But you? Pauli, I can't bear it. What is to happen? All is lost. Don't sacrifice yourself, Pauli, don't.'

'All is not lost until it is lost. We can still do something. Those of us who understand have to do something. There is no choice. My God, I'm sorry I can't come with you.'

Determination strengthened his voice as if it were announcing to an arena, not his wife, and stubbornness stemmed his grief. It was swallowed up on purpose. My heart swelled. Mother looked up and smiled a very slight smile. There were tears in her eyes. Poor, poor, mother. But Papa is right. Purpose enlarges us. I could see Mama was afraid and who could blame her? We are all afraid. Mama knew him too well to argue with such a speech but anxiety got the better of her.

'But you, a Social Democrat – that's just as dangerous, they've had you once.'

'I'll be careful, very careful. I have left the party, anyway. There is no point in being a member any more. It is better not to have those alliances.'

'But it isn't just you, your safety will depend upon others.' She spoke the words through a mouth almost closed with tension.

'Oh ye of little faith!'

'You're so stubborn, Pauli. I can't bear to leave you – think of us!'

'I do. Isn't that a good part of the reason for staying? It is our country that is falling to the ravenous beasts.'

His voice rose again slightly – there is the power of something other in it at such moments.

'I cannot go alone with Franziska, it isn't possible, Pauli.'

'There is no choice, my dear one. You have so much to give. If you stay it will all be destroyed. In any case, I cannot guarantee your safety now if you stay. I could never forgive myself if you were arrested. I have found someone who can secure your exit visas.'

I nodded to myself as I crept away, my heart thumping. I couldn't watch Mama's tears in case they got inside me. Papa is right. I lay awake thinking in circles. I have Bertie's letters under my pillow. I will not run away to England just because my dead grandma was a Jew. I will not leave Bertie to fight this terrible monster alone.

I waited until they had gone to bed. They retired so silently. No chatter, no laughter as so often after a performance. Sorrow drags their heels now, silences their words. The sorrow of parting, of bad dreams hovering, but as yet not unfolded. Fräulein Niemeier's twisted face would not let me sleep. I crept down to the study to read what Papa had been reading. I had to know, but my all-consuming curiosity was edged with foreboding.

There was a book on father's desk by Herr Hitler. I knew I was about to look into the thoughts of the dragon which was puffing up its strength, ready to breathe the fires of terror over our nation. Jews are being picked off the streets – Mama's friend in the theatre, Herr Fuchs had Jewish relations. Is that why he was taken away? Jews are not allowed to work in the theatre any more. Life is so full of terrible mysteries now. Bertie will never be able to sit beneath the apple tree with me with two blue eyes and a smooth, unbroken face. I must see him again soon. They cannot send me away. I will stand with him against this threatening tide of hatred.

I saw things in those pages which Fräulein Niemeier had seen and which must have put the poison on her tongue. Now she is spitting it out upon her world and ours and she doesn't even know it is pure poison.

My curious fingers strayed to a paper screwed up on the burnt-out embers of the fire – a letter from Bertie. I flattened it on the floor and seeing what it was, wondered that it had not been burnt immediately after it was read. Papa is not usually careless. He'd just screwed it up and left it there. Is it because Mama is going away?

'Two more of our people arrested. We have traced them to the prison camp at Dachau. No reasons given. K's printing press was smashed – remember the last pamphlet? He's gone into hiding. The Gestapo found out. They got no names, thank God, but who knows what they have on their list? They have paid informers everywhere. This letter will be delivered to you personally – we must never trust the mail again. Dear Friend, I don't need to tell you to be prudent. It has always been you who has had to rein me in. Keep the little one safe at all costs, and your dear wife. You know what I am saying. Hatred is contagious and many already seem to have little or no immunity to it. Dangerously blind eyes are everywhere. They are trading on fear: that will never be our downfall. Destroy this letter immediately, of course! Never let the Gestapo get the better of us. Ever yours, Bertholdt.'

It was as if my head was lifted into a cloud as I read the last line and I became something more than I am as little me, a German schoolgirl. I too, shall not be afraid.

I struck a match and watched the letter burn, then took a piece of writing paper from the desk and wrote to Bertie, just two lines:

I will stay for you and all you stand for. I am not afraid.

Your Franziska

My head was light as I sealed the envelope. The sealing had some special significance because the letter was an oath. I cannot undo it. It is final. I prayed to the Creator for peace of mind, but did not sleep until the dawn. And when I slept, I dreamt I went to a beautiful garden and it was filled with beings who were pure light. When I woke, I woke in the very arms of tranquillity.

October 20th, 1934

Mama has been sorting through all her belongings in the last two weeks. It makes me feel uneasy, but I am resigned to the inevitable. Life is never going to be the same again. When I am agitated, I remember the tranquillity of those hours two-and-a-half weeks ago. Sometimes, when I reach for it, it comes like a blessing and it lifts me out of time. I sit in the window and merge with the trees, the grass, the flowers and the birds – most of all the birds as they fly their freedom high above all this enclosing dark.

I had been to a friend's that morning and we had been unable to talk because there were other girls present from families different from ours. I came back feeling uncomfortable. I tried to escape the feeling and I was sitting like that, so still, when Mama's voice broke the stillness and I almost jumped out of my quarter-Jewish skin.

'Franzi, come, we have a very special lunch waiting. Afterwards the three of us are going to drive out to the country to Aunt Isabelle's. It's a special day, my darling.'

The almost hysterical note of excitement in her voice was forced, nervous.

'Where have you been? You never tell us where you are. You are always in some distant place, darling. Come, come.'

I tried to listen, to relate her words to myself, to translate. I walked through water into the dining room, half knowing what I would hear. Our old maid looked at me very quizzically from under her heavy eyebrows. The old one doesn't say very much but I think she understands me more than anyone in her own way. She observes. She never gives opinions nor tries to mould the world to her design. She waits and listens, faithfully. I could have sworn I read pity when her eyes turned to Mama.

The wild mushrooms and buttered broccoli tasted as delicious as the best asparagus. How did our dear Birgit manage to find such food in these difficult times? She is very clever to get such foods for us all. Mama, her black luxuriant hair piled high, gold earrings flashing, declared, 'We will talk of a special surprise this afternoon, Franzi.' I admired her beautifully tailored mulberry suit but said nothing.

Papa was silent, a faint smile flickering across the question mark of his face. His brows were raised, his chin lowered – benign, yet intense, sunk into his red-brown flecked tweed jacket. I looked into the tortoiseshell patterns of his waistcoat buttons, tracing their brown smudged swirls as mother chattered on in a whirlpool of words which had no power to suck me in. Already I was a bird, flying to Bertie, carrying his message.

They didn't know that I was already a messenger. When I realized what was happening, I went to his friend Fritz, who I had met here in our house, and pleaded. I need to become indispensable to him.

When he finds out, he will be so pleased with me. I have been to the station, fetched packets, delivered to strange addresses, in dark basements in poor areas and houses in middle-class streets. I don't look over my shoulder. The light puts a shield around me, so the Gestapo will not know me. They will never see me. I am walking in measured steps, not hurrying too much, as if on a precipice, a letter in my pocket. Fritz with his thick spectacles, so dedicated, so fanatical. His questions when we met came at me like hailstones until fatigue forced tears to the backs of my eyes, but I fought on until he called me safe. My reward was a task, not a smile. Declared perfect for the job, looking so young and innocent, and he said, 'You know the value of silence'. I am never allowed to acknowledge him in a public place should chance ever throw us like dice together in a café, a crowd or an empty street. It has actually happened twice. The first time I was startled, but I remembered the rules and hoped the friends at my table saw no change in my face. Fritz had seen me, but looked straight through me as if I were a stranger. It is a strange feeling, this safety in pretended alienation – the very thing we are hoping to stem in our country.

'But Darling, where *are* you? Such a dreamer. You must be in love.' A hot dart flashed down my body, electric, like fear.

Mama caught her breath and put her hand to her mouth as if she had said something wrong. Papa smiled.

I fought a hot flush and tore a piece of bread, then coughed, pretending I had swallowed awkwardly.

Mama looked concerned but, thank God, when I stopped and smiled, she laughed and our maid came in with a beautiful cheesecake smothered in dark cherries preserved in brandy from late spring from Aunty's cherry tree. There was a faint air of hysteria around our dear leading player. Mama clapped her hands. 'How beautiful. Just look at this! Franzi, Pauli, look! Look!' – as if we had never seen cheesecake before.

I admired her child-like joy, her freshness. She was always such fun, her joy and her tears so full, so consuming, larger than life, always on the stage. How could Mama live without an audience? How could she live without the characters and the words which came alive through her and were her very life-blood?

'Come on, Birgit, take a piece for yourself, then be a dear and bring us some good strong coffee to brace us for our journey.' She handed Birgit a plate with a generous helping and not waiting for thanks or the maid's departure to the kitchen, she turned and smiled a wrinkled smile at me. Her eyes were dancing. 'A *large* piece for you Pauli. You must build your strength and for you, Franzi, you are a growing girl and me, a small little piece because I must consider my figure.'

Another dart hit me in the solar plexus. I would not let the insisting, pressing tears burn the backs of my eyes. Instead, I laughed nervously and picked at the cherries, their juice as red as blood in the snow-white cream-cheese and Bertie's lonely eye winked at me as if he were there with us in our dining room.

The silence was a heavy dull hum all the way to Aunty's place.

Everyone had withdrawn into their own thoughts, anxieties and obstinacies. I cried for them, my parents, just a little, a tear or two, alone in the back seat of my father's car on that misty yellow October afternoon. And then I thought of Birgit's swollen hips and wondered if cheesecake stained with cherry juice, red as blood, gave her solace amidst her quiet thoughts, like her well-kept larder, forever waiting.

Frances is entangled with lives she feels she must honour in her screenplay. Will she be able to do justice to these unsung heroes, bring them sufficiently to life to reach hearts and minds, as well as drawing an audience?

As she puts her pen down, she realises she has been up for four hours.

From her window the morning appears still and closed in. Mist hangs heavily over the lawns, clings to the trees. The hills have disappeared. Frances suffocates. Life stagnates in her. She cannot move into the day.

'Frances, we are always waiting. The bus will come and go – and the next one ... *There is a tide in the affairs of man, which taken at the flood, leads on to fortune, omitted ...*'

Joe's voice sounds threatening, despite his humour aligning Shakespeare's momentous warning with catching school buses.

Numbed, Frances is waiting for the suffering to pass. Joe goes on harrying her.

'If you can't beat it, join it. Welcome to the world. Will you deign to honour us with your company?' he quips.

Joe often harries her. She needs and despises this when the torpor descends. But he has no power to dispel the moods which descend on her.

'We don't even know where the dogs are.' She gathers up her mail, crumples the junk and hears trees creek and squeal somewhere in her mind as they are felled for all this paper. Her soul cries out for simplicity.

'Better not to know.' Joe is pragmatic as he takes the mail with its appalling messages of overwhelming tragedy away from her and goes to throw it away, unread.

Uncertainty and longing has hold of her. She wants to gather up these stolen waifs, keep them safe, spirit them away to some yearned-for and forgotten peaceable kingdom.

The boys run in pulling on their jackets. 'Bye, Mum!' they shout. Frances calls out her goodbye and waves as Joe checks their kit and sees them to the door. He comes back frowning.

'You could help.' Joe is irritated as he clears away cats' breakfast dishes. 'Dot will be here soon.' Frances wants to stop him.

'She can't get through everything.' He splashes hot water over clinking stainless steel, showing his irritation.

Joe won't let her explore the depths, but occasionally, when she does, she comes back with a pearl. When daily life baffles him, it overrules the fact that he knows there is a price for everything in this world. Maybe he would write something which really moved people to tears if he could, she thinks, but dares not say.

Yesterday evening Frances helped the boys with some homework, cleaned the cat dishes, the dog dishes, scrubbed the kitchen table, swept away the trail of animal debris. Joe hadn't noticed, or has forgotten. Frances cleaned every speck away, searching for the sparkle of perfection.

She doesn't answer him, but clears some dead flowers and goes to pick new ones in the garden: Yellow chrysanthemums. She wonders at them, smelling them. They are strong flowers and cannot be called sweet, but pleasant; they carry the edge of the year in them; the sadness of autumn's closing shutters. The world turns, turns from the sun to return. All things return. She'll take the flowers to her desk, to help illumine her thoughts.

At her desk, she writes, Dear Dog, we cannot be parted. Maybe I should have insisted on keeping you. I could have avoided this pining, this waiting, these hanging days, having to rely on faith. These taunting days. But I did what others told me was best and have to trust their judgement.

We are the resistance and resistors have to resist their fears, their impatience and any desires for instantaneous relief.

As a dog, you can teach me what is simple and best and restore my faith in tomorrow. That is how dogs are.

Teach me to look upon horizons as if they were a part of me and not some distant dream which might recede with my approach.

Teach me the joy of forgiveness, of a world without bitterness. Teach me the joy of a wagging tail and a world without analysis.

Teach me to leap and jump without falling, to run with the wind as if the world were the wind and I the wind and the world.

Teach me one-ness without resistance and the will to be at one with every given moment as if it were as precious as the Life which breathes us, you and I and the others.

Chapter 6

Frances forces herself to set the dog aside, feeling compelled to return to Franziska, who is always waiting for her, beckoning from the black ink on white pages, neatly piled together upon the wine-red table. Beckoning. Silently. Insistently.

Waiting. All Germany, poised upon the brink of madness is waiting.

October, 1934
So, this was the goodbye to Aunt Isabelle. They thought I would accept more readily if the proposed departure was announced in the presence of my aunt. They know how close we are, how she understands me. Why were they so afraid? Had she told them something of Bertie? Had Papa seen something I had not known he'd seen?

We sat surrounded by the heavy oak and mahogany furniture – pieces which looked as if they would last forever; the elaborate carvings on the chest, the waxy perfumed smell of polish, the glow from the fire and the heavy curtains closed against the gusty rain of an autumn evening which shouted of winter marching close behind. Caught between this still, inner solidity and the outer tempest, Mama was pressing with too many words.

'But there is no question about it, Franzi, no question.'

Her hand fluttered through the air like a frightened bird held by a cord. 'You are such a proud child, so aloof at times. It's as if you do not hear us. See how she holds her head so high, her shoulders so straight. My child. My child!'

'Be sensible, Franzi, you are an intelligent girl.' Father spoke in quiet, measured tones. Their anxiety closed in upon me.

'Leave the child. Let her think it over quietly.' Aunty was validating my individuality but by the time she spoke I was already far removed from the room and the voices and the fears. My head had been lifted up and my body was without shape, form or measurement. The walls disappeared and I seemed to be gazing into an open landscape that never ended.

I was looking from far away and heard those dear voices of concern as echoes from some distant land. I cannot tell how long I remained there, but when I returned, Mama was talking about clothes. Papa had dozed off in a chair by the fire and the subject of England had been suspended.

November 4th, 1934

Mama leaves tomorrow. I went to the hairdresser and had my hair cut short and dyed light copper brown and powdered my face to look pale. A stranger to myself, I am on the train to Leipzig. Truly believing I would go with her; Mama had packed so many things for me. I made up my small suitcase from those large ones and left while she was out shopping.

The letter I have left her is a simple one, telling how I cannot go with her to England, but that she *must* go, otherwise all our lives may be ruined, that my mind is made up, that there is a task for me here, that is mine alone and not even her love could persuade me from it; that I am a wayward child of fate who lives in and out of this dream of life.

The train clatters in my head, in and out, in and out, going on, going on, going on: I already live a life you do not know, Mama.

Our paths part awhile, but love can never be lost. It crosses worlds and aeons and flies.

It rises from the ashes of loves torn and broken. It is a phoenix and a sun. It is the immortal in us. Do not look back, Mama.

Do not look for me. We have been and are to be in many different guises, but that which is truly us never changes. Let Heine speak for me:

>*I love thee still,*
>*And, fell this world asunder,*
>*My love's eternal flame would rise*
>*Midst chaos, crash and thunder!*

Mama mine, go safely and be well.

I go to meet whatever God has in store for me, head high and with a sure step. God and Grandma will watch over us.

Your Franziska, always.

I know there is chaos, crash and thunder ahead, but I know too, that souls are eternal and that we are each one in the hands of our Creator as if we were his only care. I close my eyes because I do not want to see Mama's tears. I listen to the clatter of the train because I cannot listen to her distress. The words in the letter came to me from the air. It was as if my hand wrote apart from my head so that my own words were a surprise to me.

I have also written to Papa telling him the plans must not be changed and so I cannot go to Bertie until after Mama has left, because he is sure to try and contact him and I cannot force him to lie:

Dearest Papi,
Do not let Mama delay. She gave me dreams; you gave me beliefs and the strength to live them. Now they are truly mine. I am doing with them what I must do. Do not fear. I will be back in a while. With love always, Franziska.
P.S. Please do not try to change anything.

I left Mama a last red rose which I had found in the garden, curled tight and deep as wine velvet. I broke the thorns from its stem so that its love should not chance to give her pain.

November 5th, 1934

I am staying the night in a strange little *Gasthof* reading some poetry and trying to keep warm. The large lady who keeps this place looked at me and shook her head at the fact that I did not want a large dinner, and refused her greasy *Spiegeleier* and *Speck*. She tried to ask questions about why I am alone here and I feel I must hide in my room, too frightened to leave. I saw her chatting away with a group of SA when I returned from a walk, her beer and *schnapps* firing their raucous laughter, her red cheeks redder from cooking their *bratwurst* and her jowls flapping at their crude jokes. I feel very alone. It is a test of my courage. I hide my head under the pillows not to hear the noise below, glad that the address I am going to is in my head and not written on paper. How shall I survive her breakfast? I will go without. 'My name is written in water.' Those words have so many meanings now.

November 9th, 1934

Here I am at Bertie's latest address, but despite my hunger and former airiness my whole body has suddenly become a dead weight. He is not here.

Never stay too long in one place, is one of the rules. The woman who lives here says he will be back soon, but exactly *when* is not known and she cannot say where he has gone.

My father's name was my passport to enter. I spend my days trying to be useful, but it is hard being amongst people where one is unknown, where everyone is so watchful.

We must not even go out into the street together. I have been counting and packing leaflets all day. The place smells of ink and bare wooden boards and dust. I feel grey. Everything creaks. People are jumpy. Creaks make us jump. We are hidden away in an annexe behind a grocery shop. Here I am no longer someone's precious child. So much intensity. I do not speak except when necessary, I observe. I try to fit in. All my movements are painfully jerky. I feel like a little grey mouse and traps are set – and no cheese. If only Bertie were here. If only this were another time, another place, another world!

I should very much like to hear Papa's voice, but dare not telephone him. I go to bed exhausted from the tension of being a stranger in a group already stretched tight with the strain of living on the outside of life. I take an hour to get to sleep, praying nothing will break.

November 10th, 1934

This evening we all went at different times, by different ways, to the home of Frau X, a well-off, middle-aged lady who helps to fund the work. All of the people present were dissidents, including a priest who spoke with fire about the treatment of the Jews, how they have been expelled from the professions. It is a great excitement to be amongst such people, eyes open, vital with ideas.

Perhaps we shall yet turn the tide in this country of ours. There was an atmosphere of optimism and some relaxation as we sipped white wine from Mainz. But M, in whose apartment Bertie is currently lodging, told me it is not the same when he is away. I think he leads and they follow. Frau X, large-boned and beautifully dressed in soft purple crêpe, has something inside her which makes me believe she could hold back an army with a single gesture. I fell asleep comforted.

November 11th, 1934

I keep these papers in a false bottom to my suitcase. It's my father's bag; I'm sure he made it like this himself. It is so perfectly done that no-one would ever know. I never told him I knew of its existence. Sometimes doubts creep in when I leave ajar the door which guards my faith and then it seems these pages should be burnt. But another voice speaks louder and tells me to keep this record. I ask the angels every night and morning to keep it safe.

I could not even tell my best friend that I was coming here.

M is a restless spirit, who goes to sleep late and rises early, but is utterly absorbed in her work so that smiles waft across her face like a random breeze and disappear as quickly, her thoughts blown far away into our threatened future. She has agreed that Papa will not be informed of my presence should he telephone here during the first week. He has not done so. This is strange. Is he safe? Perhaps he feels it is far from safe to telephone. What if he has been arrested again? What if Bertie never comes back? Can I face this alone any longer? I am trying to reach the mountain-tops, but I see only dark clouds. I pray they shall not engulf me.

November 13th, 1934

It was about eleven o'clock yesterday evening. I was reading and then the voice broke into the story as if I had suddenly been transported into a dream-place, everything unreal.

I heard M's voice replying, 'All right. All well.' And then she said, 'You have a young visitor.' 'Yes?' Surprise, question in the voice and I burst through the door...

'Dear God!' he said. 'Franziska!' and more quietly and slowly, as if he had considered then, almost a whisper, 'Franziska.' There was a tight smile on his face, a puzzlement, a shock... 'But how did you come here? Does your father know?' All of a sudden, I felt put into that place again where I no longer wanted to be. I was glad M was turning to leave us. I would not be a child any more.

'No, no! Not at all. He doesn't know. It was the only way...'

He closed his eye as if I was perhaps a handful of trouble and my heart stopped dead. I shrank and all the tightness, sorrow, anxiety and grief of the last days wanted to burst out in a river of tears, but I contorted my face to stop them, twisting every last muscle to control the threatened flood. At this, he put his long arms around my waist, lifted me in the air, swung me around once, squeezed hard, and said, 'Let's get some good hot coffee and talk'. He smiled at my dyed hair, called me 'Hothead' and stroked it while the water boiled and the night outside the kitchen window was still and glinting with frost in the moonlight, but my face was burning and we sat in his room and talked until dawn and I fell asleep in his arms, on the floor before the fire, the smell of his thick tweed jacket full in my nose and the fire burning and a new day promised by the dawn chorus as if all the bells of heaven rang and I could sleep safely, Bertie's big heart pulsing, beating through my sleep for us all.

I slept until noon. I woke to see Bertie in the doorway, smiling, holding coffee which he poured for us both.

Watching him I could not help the tears which came to my eyes, silent tears for that once beautiful broken face, for such a sacrifice at the hands of ignorance and hatred.

'Are you sure you won't miss your Mama too much?' His head leaned to one side in enquiring concern.

I shook my head, but could not speak my thoughts. I composed myself – he wouldn't let me join the work if I was just a weak girl.

'I know what you have been doing for Fritz, you are a very naughty girl.' He was smiling.

'I was afraid you might say no.'

'You've obviously been doing it well – but the danger...'

'I'm very careful. I know the rules.'

'You'll have to go back to Berlin, Franzi, and study – study languages, French, English, maybe Russian – and typing.'

'Why those things?'

'It may prove useful.'

'I'd like to stay with you a little longer.'

'That would be wonderful, young lady, but only a few days. We cannot be in any one place too long. People must not be seen together. You know the rules.'

'With Papi?'

'You're his daughter.'

'But, I'm, I'm, I want to help *you*.'

The coffee was strong, warm and bitter on my tongue. I drank it as if it were nectar.

'You are stubborn too! Do you want to take a package on the train this afternoon – an hour and a half's journey?'

'Yes, yes,' I was thrilled that he felt able to employ me in this way.

'No, I shouldn't let you do it,' he was having serious second thoughts.

'But you have to now, I insist. Don't be so horrible as to refuse me,' I said.

At this point we put our arms around each other and sat, silent, for a long age, feeling each other's warmth in the face of the cold unknown.

I carried the package inside a bag of groceries on the train and calmly ate a cheese sandwich as two loud SS men stopped to look in as they walked past. No one in the compartment even looked up. The print in the magazine I was reading blurred before my eyes. I know the Gestapo check peoples' papers on trains. I read random words which slipped across the page. I did not know what was in the packet – the rules – but I knew that the printed words in there would mean arrest. Bertie's broken face. He never told me how. I felt a glance at my legs which burned me and then ice as I heard guttural chuckles – the words lost in the ice. The soothing clatter of the train as the footsteps faded. I frowned with pretended concentration but the stony faces in the carriage took no interest in my presence.

I pulled a scarf over my face and clipped each rationed word when I delivered the parcel to a woman with dark hair and bright eyes and did not accept her invitation to stay for some tea. Instead, looking carefully to see I had not been followed, I went straight to a café – by a memorized route and enjoyed the lightness of freedom from the package which had felt like a bomb in my bag. But I could not sit for long. Every precious minute away from Bertie is so much wasted time. Besides, I was eager to tell him of its safe delivery. Another knife thrust in the dragon's side – or a pinprick, but a poisoned pin, all the same, that would reach into a vein somewhere, somehow . . . somehow. I powdered my face pale again in the women's room, looked into my own dark eyes which secretly whispered 'Jew', threw back my shoulders and marched out into the rain stiff and proud as a Hitler youth maiden and made for the station at a pace which would not be noticed by curious or idle eyes.

November 20th, 1934
A week has passed as quickly as a brown-stubble cornfield flashing by the window of a train, every sense longing to savour, drink in, and yet it was snatched in a moment, but not before it had leapt in, become a part of body and soul. This last week could be a fleeting gasp or a lifetime. It is both. The sadness is that it is finished, as finished as a breath breathed out and become part of the earth's breath. The joy is that no matter where I am, I can rest cradled in Bertie's arms, knowing that the communion of two so well met protects from all that threatens in a world where love itself is twisted and choked, taunted and made lame.

'Jude unerwunscht.' I passed the sign outside the mean-looking restaurant denying entry to Jews, one my mother would disdain to go in even if the very wolves of hunger were gnawing at her stomach. She would not look twice at the doorstep, she of flashing beauty, raven-haired and dark-lit eyes. I see the smile lines at their corners. Who could not smile with them? What ignorant beast has pushed that scorching talent from the stage?

'I have to leave now, *Liebling*.' The voice which woke me was quiet, but urgent. 'Go back to your Papa in Berlin. He will be home again tomorrow.' It was already 11.30 at night. I had just fallen asleep. 'Come to Frau I's house, then take the first train tomorrow.'

'Why now?' I asked, wide awake. The suddenness of the announcement had stunned me.

'Don't ask too many questions, please, for your own sake. I shall not be here again. Moving on. Let's pack your things, quickly, little flower.'

I was wide awake now. 'Can't I come with you?'

'No. It's a long journey, difficult things. Go back to Berlin. Your father will take care of you. He knows what to do.'

'You have spoken to him, then?'

'A message came. Lisalotte is safely in England.' 'Mama.' I said the word quietly, in gratitude and respect.

He took hold of me by the shoulders, looked into my eyes with his strong blue eye, 'Thank God,' he said. '*Gott sei Dank*.' His hands so tense and strong, shaking me a little as if he were trying to shake sense into a little fool and as if he were in two minds about what the little fool was doing. Silent thunder roared in my head, blocking out all questions, all answers.

We packed, quickly. He moved with quiet calm as if we had to catch a train to go on holiday, not as if the SS might hammer down the door at any moment. He picked up my little perfume bottle, put a little on my wrist, smelt it with one long breath, smiled, put his hands on my hair, and said,

> *E'en as a lovely flower,*
> *So fair, so pure . . .*

and I thought for a moment that he would cry.

'. . . That God may keep thee,' he whispered as he packed the bottle away. 'You will come and see us?'

'When and if it is possible. You know they have prisons and camps waiting for people like us. The trick is to keep going and slip through their nets, my little silver fish.' He spoke almost flippantly now as if we were playing a game.

'Go to your studies. You can then do some translations for us. OK?'

'Whatever you say.'

'Pauli will direct you. He is a good father. I think he has already forgiven you.'

'Now, quickly. I will take you to Frau I's house before I leave.' M was not there. They had gone to pack up the printed material. The workshop would be left quite empty. No trace of us would remain.

'What has happened?' I asked him, daring to break the silence as we drove to Frau I's. It was my first real emergency. I had to know.

Bertie didn't want to answer.

'You went to the café, stayed twenty minutes. Walked the long way to the station?'

'Of course. As you directed.'

'Nothing suspicious on the journey?' I told him of the SS on the train.

He nodded. 'When you delivered the parcel, did you show yourself? Did you go in?'

'I wore tinted glasses, a headscarf and a woollen scarf around my chin – and I spoke through the scarf with a different voice. I clipped the words. Not even my dyed hair could be seen.'

'Thank God.' He sighed heavily. 'No one looked at you in the café?'

'She has been arrested.' I knew it without being told. 'God help her.' I said.

Bertie put a hand on my knee, his lips tightened together, his brow furrowed, his voice silent. The silence which followed was like those bowed silences we keep out of respect for the dead.

When we said goodbye in Frau I's dark passageway, my head felt like some empty container spinning in space, but I forced attention upon his every movement, his every word. He held my chin in his hands and smiled.

'You are a real professional. But don't get too confident. Never forget what we are relying upon.'

'Our lives depend upon one another,' I answered him, very quietly.

'We have woven a fine thread, but a strong one.'

I took courage from the confidence in his tone.

'Stay beautiful.' I heard the sorrow for his own loss in those words. I wanted to say 'And you,' but said, 'Stay strong.'

We embraced, but time and circumstance, all in a moment, draw the shutters closed and Bertie is gone into another unknown day.

November 21st, 1934

The train journey back to Berlin was uneventful enough, but I have learnt to be watchful at all times while everyone around me seems content to be practically blind. There were brownshirts hanging around the station, but I didn't even glance their way. I am learning how to be anonymous, to face the other way, unnoticed when inside I feel like a walking target for their anger. But sometimes I feel the light, as if I am moving inside a misty cloud.

The house is very quiet without Mama. I miss her; her smiles, her laughter, her singing and now I must have made her sad. Will she laugh and sing here again?

Papa has not come back yet, but I push anxiety aside when it creeps out to tug at me. Dear old Birgit made a fuss at seeing me and is most unusually talkative. Where have I been? Why is my hair a different colour? 'Your poor mother, going away alone,' and so on. Is it all the disturbance which is provoking her to speak words which would normally stay sealed behind those faded blue eyes?

But I answer her with fake cheerfulness that I went to stay with an old school friend, that I need to get on with my studies and hope she is satisfied with my smiles. She'll surely be content with simple answers. She doesn't have an enquiring mind. She is more concerned to make cheesecake, but I tell her, 'No, no, there is no cause for celebration – perhaps when Papa gets back, should he want it.' She has gone to light the fire in his study, to keep it ready for him. Perhaps I am being unkind. Birgit needs to feel we need her and we do, but just to think of rich food makes me feel ill.

Where is Bertie now? What of the woman who was arrested? I fear to write these things, but I will hide his notebook away again, where they will be safe from the faces which come all too alive in the darkest hours. Maybe Papa will know where Bertie is, even if he dare not tell. I cannot live endless days without knowing . . .

November 21st, 1934. Midnight
A message came this afternoon. Someone took a risk, putting it through the door, not knowing, perhaps, if our maid was reliable. She has never been tested. These are different times. I cannot simply count on her. She mustn't see my notes. She said she opened the door to look for the messenger after she saw the letter come through. A young man was hurrying away. She was wearing a puzzled frown as she related this. I have a rendezvous tomorrow in the *Kurfurstendam*. There is urgency in the summons – it must be important. Why did the messenger not ask for me personally? Are they inexperienced? Bertie has insisted we must always be looking out for traps. I will have to consult Papa.

Surely, he'll be back? I have turned the paper over and over in my hands, trying to feel it, but nothing comes because I am thinking of Bertie and I am fighting this foolish weakness.

God keep Bertie and Papa safe. I must not, cannot, question what I am doing here, but I am cold and alone and unsure of this moment in which I stand, let alone tomorrow, yet life will push me through its door.

Chapter 7

Frances sets Franziska's notes aside. She knows this too well – being pushed through the door of tomorrow. Joe never seems to baulk at tomorrow. For him, it is always a welcome opportunity, an invitation to some new, exciting place to which he walks with sure and steady footsteps.

Of sanguine disposition, he is far from understanding the range of Frances' melancholic nature. Her minor key moves him, but cannot encompass him. He can dissect it with an acuity which astounds her, yet he cannot feel it in his heart and so can never reach her. This he also knows and that is why he will organize his working day so that he finishes in time to be ready for the boys when they get home from school, to cook dinner for the family, to allow Frances time to meander amidst the wild gardens of her soul and devote what is left to the campaigns which eat into her, crushing and darkening the colour which longs to burst through.

Frances walks with the dogs while Joe makes dinner. He's quick, doesn't have to think about the task, while Frances prefers to think and think how the script will have to be, and striding through the long grass, can't stand apart from Franziska, who shadows each step as if it were her own.

At dinner, the youngest of the dogs jumps up on to a chair, takes a place and puts a paw on the table, whimpering slightly, asking puppy-child-like to join in with dinner. No one complains, but no one puts a hot piece of spicy potato into his mouth. He puts his chin on the table appealing, expecting responses. He gets amused attention.

Windrush, a small scruffy shaggy tabby rescued from a carrier bag left in a London telephone box, nestles into an untidy schoolboy lap as if the world were blissfully comfortable and offers only comfort on into an opulently provident everlasting moment. The telephone box trauma is utterly dissolved by present contentment.

The dog jumps down, sniffs insistently at a school blazer flung across a chair.

'Something interesting in there?' Joe looks at his youngest child who shrugs. He's forgotten the sandwich remains, a week old, going grey in their sweating polythene bag.

The eldest complains that his RE teacher won't discuss the Fall. 'What's his excuse?' Frances wants to know.

'This is not a subject which falls within our current curriculum.' The boy imitates the man and makes them laugh.

'Did you insist?' she asks.

'I said that if we stuck entirely to what's laid down, we might come out like parrots knowing very little of any real worth.'

Frances and Joe exchange a smile at their son's precocious pedantry. 'What did he say to that?'

'You naughty boy. Be quiet, you naughty boy.' The caricature of the inadequate Father Malise always makes for hilarity.

'The poor man can't be expected to wade out of his depth.' Joe doesn't know why he's defending him. He wants teachers who stretch and provoke their young minds to a point where creativity floods them, sends them careering into new and wonderful worlds.

'Father Malises's got bad breath and he squirms around the girls, especially the blonde ones,' pipes up the owner of the mouldy sandwiches, while Windrush attempts to make good her young human's neglect of soap and water with her sandpaper tongue. Frances watches as her son fondles the creature – a communication so complete, silent, innocent, with no demands.

'Creeping around in those sinister long black robes – they say everything about what the Church has done to real spiritual teachings.'

Frances feels defeated by the enormity of the Church's betrayal of true Christianity, true compassion.

'Black makes light negative – it sucks it all in and makes it as if it doesn't exist,' says Windrush's best friend.

'But the smallest light diminishes the blackness,' Frances counters.

'Yes but if you have blackout blinds, they suck all the light from the room.'

'True,' Joe says. 'Is this because you don't like darkness?'

'Yes.'

He always sleeps with the light on, Frances is thinking. It is our primordial fear of the dark. 'There's always light somewhere.' Joe smiles, clearing one or two things from the table.

Frances sits back in her chair and smiles indulgently at her fair offspring. She has what Franziska was never allowed. At this moment, she mourns her heroine, yet feels she can truly say, 'I am happy'. She looks and listens as they chat with their father and wants to freeze-frame the moment. No lump, just the fullness of contentment in her throat now. The air rests upon her chest as if she had just awoken from deep refreshing sleep to a dappled sunlit morning.

When these moments come, she knows that life is a precious gift not to be wasted, that despair is an enemy which sickens, that it is such times as this which sustain, recall us when we wander off unaware into life's darker alleys. Their old deerhound lays its face on the table. Frances runs a finger along the smooth con tour of its forehead, then cups its skull in her hand to share the moment. 'Dear Dog,' she whispers. 'Soon.'

Soon they will curl up together on the old velvet sofa, a comfortable heap, sharing warmth and friendship like creatures everywhere in their burrows, holes and nests.

Later, cupped in the hand of a gentle night, the house is held in the stillness of peace.

'We are one another.' The phrase drifts to and fro in the quiet of Frances's mind; a lullaby closing another day which has been both a moment and an eternity, drifting into sleep which marks no time except by its ending. 'Restore us,' is the appeal she mouths as it takes them, human and creature, one by one.

Tomorrow the blank pages will demand further explanation to help restore a balance lost long ago. Tomorrow already points its finger at the blankness and demands she use the means she has to help make restoration.

Tomorrow, whatever it may ask, whether or not it will be heard, will always come and seek us out, each one, and just as we entered yesterday's end, we shall enter tomorrow's beginning quite alone and yet in the company of hosts unseen, beckoning, beckoning. Frances knows because she sees with eyes others do not know they possess.

Looking over her shoulder at yesterday, Frances starts out on the morning longing for a simplicity which eludes her as she waves the boys goodbye. Soon, she takes comfort in the dog whose head rests on her feet as she begins to write, the other snoring softly, comfortably replete with breakfast, in a corner.

The day is open with sunlight as Frances sits at her table. She knows she should be addressing Franziska, but her thoughts go elsewhere.

Dear Dog, being governed simply by Nature's laws, you are not caught up with troubled questions, recriminations, reflections. Your emotions, the same as ours, as any careful observer can see, and as the careless demonstrate so inadequately with electrodes and dissections, are not twisted in the rippled mirror of taunting reason which leads, but does not by itself fulfil.

There are moments when the illusion fades to reveal a bright reality beyond this time and space. But being moments, they are quickly sucked into the swirling currents of life, bright jewels which might catch the sun rays of other minds awakening.

I wish you rays of sunlight to lie in, your eyes half closed in a pleasure of their life-giving caress.

On the 21st Joe told me not to go to the extraordinary little meeting. His helpless anxiety grew perceptibly as I turned from thought to thought, ducking from under his arms, unconvinced. He warned it would take too much out of me. I decided, as usual, at the very last moment and agonized all day over the decision.

Indecision and being swayed by others more determined, that is a weakness I'm fighting to overcome.

How do we change old, bad habits which sit so obstinately in the worn pathways of the brain? It is a formidable problem. Humans and animals find it hard. 'Familiar', even if it is problematical or perhaps dangerous, is easier, just as usual, even if unwise, is 'secure'. We cling to the familiar just as we clung, helpless babes, instinctively, to our mothers when the world was still an unfamiliar place. Even mothers of dead cloth or spiked steel . . . And everyone has seen them, those wretched monkey babies, clinging instinctively, no different from our own – mothers made by professors with letters of licence stuck like labels after their names, letters we are supposed to admire, letters of learned indifference.

I went to discuss the plans, of course, but arrived a little late – almost certainly as a result of resistance to going at all – and contributed nothing. There were two people who had not been invited, but Pamela, surprisingly, did not question their presence and did not even ask how they knew about the meeting. Secrets are not easily kept in the movement.

Those two did not stand apart, but barely spoke. One was the wife of one of the senior office staff, Steve Lawton. He always kept an odd silence, never smiled, underlined his signature and, at twenty-seven, was beginning to look pale and grey beneath the eyes. Perhaps it was the lack of humour which gave a sense of unease about him. She was large and loud, with a haphazardly cropped mop of mousy curls. She vibrated outward, smiling, but there was a hollow ring. There was a distinct sense that if prodded, the apparent convictions would burst, like a puffball, dispersing, scattering on the wind.

When she put her arm around someone, was she saying, 'I want to be a generous person, give me a chance?' She was Pauline, alias Pinkie, of the dimpled smile and ample bosom. Bouncing, she seemed to stumble. I could not be convinced.

Her teenage companion, Sasha, worked in the office in a junior position. She had the appearance of pleasant, if not pleasing, neutrality, but whether that was for opportunistic reasons, it was hard to tell.

Suspicion is learnt where naiveté is no virtue. Her blonde heavy-fringed hair sat well upon her small-boned face; its seriousness set too hard for one such a short way into the business of living.

We, being carried towards the middle of our lives, began to feel the gap between the often unthinking, but direct enthusiasm of the young and our learned tendency to caution – a two-edged sword when dealing with the uncertain qualities of fickle humanity.

Sasha rarely offered opinions, but seemed to watch too carefully, the grey-blue eyes scanning the room with the attention of an owl that must swoop to feed when necessity demands. The dullness of her eyes drew a question in my mind, waiting as she waited. I doodled.

The room was small and stuffy, even though we were only eight. Four of our group had not yet appeared. That made us edgy. To rely upon others is nearly always to be disappointed. The room smelt of dust and stale disinfected polish. The plastic chairs were sticky. Who had found this place, I wondered? Around a scratched Formica table, we talked of commandeering evidence from the filing cabinets of criminals protected by the law, while below us, in a room far larger, to accommodate the crowd, old ladies enjoyed an hour or two out, filling their bingo cards: 'Legs eleven; go to heaven, number seven.' A different adrenaline flowing. Housey, Housey home and dry.

> *Little mousey, do not cry,*
> *I do not believe that you were born to die.*
> *By the million.*

Small fry, they gamble; brassy pound coins. Wrinkled grins. Others here were gambling with their freedom, for a prize not their own.

The room bore down on my spirits. My critical thoughts, born of anger, were discouraging. Weary and undecided, I was unsure of the rightness of the plans. Later, in a nearby café, I sipped tea too black and bitter and listening to the chatter, felt some of them should learn much more about the safety of silence. Talking can be such a noxious indulgence, and often such a false comforter.

The plan – which was not openly discussed – was to take only documents from the laboratory late on Saturday, but no animals. There would not be enough time to take both and documents are much needed evidence. That was the kind of decision which is too terrible for anyone to have to make, but it was made, and it was pointless to question further.

We would call upon the help of our trusted male friend, Rik, who was to drive the papers away in a vehicle of his own.

The public demonstration was planned to start at four, outside a separate building owned by the same company, to create noise and distraction, so that the four could go in and take whatever they could later. We had detailed plans of the building – donated by an inside informer who couldn't rise to bringing documents out herself. But we were thankful for a small mercy and that mercy was live in someone who worked in such a place.

I was tired and unable to sleep that night. The acid from the tea made me nauseous. Perhaps I had bitterness too much in mind. It was hard to put all those disparate feelings to rest, even on such a beautiful night.

My restless thoughts wandered on to the gloom ahead. I could not face the winter, I said, but would, no doubt, because, in those eternal words, spring is never far behind.

Chapter 8

Today is a bank holiday and they are taking advantage of its quietness. Joe, the boys and Frances are going to walk with the dogs in the hills all afternoon where the air is fresh and the wind blows all anxiety away.

There is a stillness over the world.

Frances feels almost as if she dare not breathe as they sit on a rock overlooking the vastness of the valley below. Something pulls tight in her chest, but will not let her weep. What is this strangeness? There has been no news. Her mind flies directionless on the air currents across the wide, open landscape.

The sheep munch the grass, ignorant of the death which will later cut them down without thanks, without a thought for how they too love their lives. Horror hangs everywhere, even on a wild hilltop, above human atmospheres, on a late summer afternoon and every little stream so pretty sparkling in the sunlight fills with the blood that will flow, with the throats that will open to the clanking of the plates on every gluttonous Sunday afternoon to follow into an horizon which can hold no hope. And on, far from these rocky Welsh hills and green valleys into sun-baked Eastern lands where throats will be slashed by even stranger hands with chanted prayers to justify the massacre of lambs, so silent and confused in their suffering.

Their dogs, sniffing-eager, high-tailed, jumping, barking, leaping, licking, circling, will not let her sink into that valley where the streams flow inevitably on, gathering their terrible cargo of pain.

Frances is thinking of Black Dog waiting to join them, to shelter within the safety of hearts which refuse to join in the collective madness, to come into their world shut out from the cruel ways of ancient man, the ignoble savage, who will not choose to change his ways.

She is always thinking of him, waiting in hiding and of the woods, the fields, the hills, and the sweet, fresh air to breathe deep, all waiting for him.

She calls into the wind with a longing:

'You should be with us now.'

Joe, anxious, hearing a requiem in the wind on the top of this ancient hill, cannot fathom the sadness which envelopes his wife like a cloud descended from the heavens to chastise their freedom and togetherness.

Running along the hilltop, the four of them with their dogs are tiny silhouettes against the skyline, encompassing the whole magnificence of this landscape to its far horizon with the heights and depths of their emotion. Driven by the wind, sharp, relentless, strong, they run and run, perhaps to escape what it calls out to them? Who shall answer? Who shall answer for all of this? Who shall be involved? Who shall dare to be awake at dawn when others slumber on in a night to which they cling as if the light would shatter them into a million pieces? Who can hear? This is no whispering breath. The curse is ancient beyond imagining.

Joe cannot catch Frances's hand. The boys are running fast, the dogs faster. The dogs must run . . . And the youngsters are not deaf – something in them is tuned to this taut note of anguish. But Joe breaks it, the crescendo in his head has all but driven him mad. Frances has led them into this place from which none can escape. He stops, speaks ordinary words to his sons, 'Hey, stop. Look at that!' His lungs heaving – he laughs to break this encircling agony. He points to the distant horizon, staggered at its beauty in the glow of the late afternoon sun. The dogs stop, look up, panting, grinning real smiles.

'First to the bottom,' he shouts, with a purpose – to leave Frances with her burden stumbling alone behind them. She knows more than his thoughts – sees beyond them. Is it raindrops, tears or the wind in her eyes? She slips on the short smooth steep grass, throws out an arm to soften the fall and no one sees. Her wrist pains, stabbing, throbbing as she walks on down, but she drinks the pain in gulps. She drinks in the sharp air and swallows hard. Perhaps she was angry at him for leaving her like this? But how much of your grief can you expect another to own? None, she tells herself and resolves on silence when she reaches them.

There's an exhausted, invigorated silence as they drive down into the sleepy country town, remote from the insistent troubles of a world too complicated to hold in their heads.

'Tea at the Grain Store?' Joe offers them the comfort of predictability, warmth, tea and scones served on red and white chequered tablecloths.

The boys' affirmative chorus says they are starving, like young birds, always noisy for the next morsel. 'It was outside little towns like these, in Germany, in the thirties that they built those places and all the normal people carried on their lives blind-eyed.'

Joe doesn't answer. Today has been enough for him. He's afraid that if he cracks, the jagged edge will strike out, undermine, let rip or fall and she doesn't deserve that and the boys shouldn't be involved.

Frances fears the shutters, that she will be left utterly alone with this. 'And Biotox – an even sleepier little town. More silent.'

The boys are piling out.

He will not answer but touches her hand. It's enough. She musters a smile. 'At least one will be with us soon – one in a million.'

Joe can't speak – there's a wild requiem chorus still crashing in his head and Frances can't hear it.

But I am chained to Time, and cannot thence depart! A stray line from Shelley drifts through Frances's brain.

With that, she packs away the sadness, slams the lid and strides into the palliation of everyday comforts and the warm prattle of family life, thankful for the cautioning hand upon her sleeve, light as a whisper, strong as a halter.

Sweet strawberry jam on crumbling home-made scones, warm tea and three familiar smiles push back the shadows, for a moment. But behind this homey scene the requiem plays on and voices that will never be hushed resound to the heavens pleading for mercy, pity, love and the company of angels in their ancient grief.

It is this which will reclaim Frances when she is driven back to the ironic comfort of her desk, looking through her study window, shored up with its solidity, its sameness, its space for her creation, for ways to transform her longing into a communion.

Dear Dog, to ease the time, I am telling the whole story for you, or at least the events and the history that has led to them as I perceive it – I know our personalities are always bound to distort. Our stories can only ever be our own.

For darkened century upon century man has endeavoured to extract the secrets of life from the violation of your kingdom, even though you are our brothers and sisters whose eyes, like ours, look upon the sun and mirror the soul within. As he sunk ever deeper into the mire of materialism, the darkness grew until a new religion of the physical ousted older gods of the spiritual world.

The Latin word 'to know' gave birth to a word which embraced the contaminated seeds of unknowing. Science, oppressed by its own intellectual weight, without the Light of spirit, compressed into a system which locked itself in by its own rules, shutting out the grandeur of a greater and more Wholesome vision. The holy Whole.

From this arose a great evil: an enduring agony imposed upon those with no power to resist. Begun as a search for knowledge, it dressed its blackness in a finery which glittered with empty offers of a world safe

– for humans – from disease and hollow dreams of immortality of the flesh.

At the darkest hour, there were some who heard the screams and saw the blood and made it their own. They reached out to your kind – and wept. They suffered for you and one, who could see the true nature of the darkness, battled against the dark powers until they took her life all too soon, but there are few that know her. The Great Anna Kingsford, my hero, a very intelligent woman, independent, a prophet, seer and pioneering vegetarian, an ancient soul returned, she studied medicine in Paris because in England it was the sole preserve of men. There amongst the vivisectors who would have felled her spirit, she suffered greatly but showed she could become a physician without a single creature being harmed. Her will and strength still towers over us.

This was a hundred and more years ago, but the battles have been many; lives have been lost in subtle, hidden ways, and the Great Battle continues.

To fight it, people must open their minds, stand together and understand who the true enemy is. There are few who perceive that it is of the Powers and Principalities of Darkness ever greedy for vulnerable human souls. All too human, our people now organize, but do not always produce good leaders. Their attacks are disseminated, but gradually, they have grown and changed. A new kind of people has arisen who risk the locked doors of a prison cell to deliver fellow beings, not of their own kind, from their hell. But there are many, who, with a similar vision, for their own reasons, nevertheless oppose them. Unless we can see into another's innermost heart, his motives are hidden and invisible.

There is a quiet revolution taking place and so the demons arm the wicked with their fears.

But it is dangerous. Even the well-intentioned humans can be tainted, led by phantom images into greyness where the faces of your kind are dimmed by the 'I' named ego which should be magnificent, but which, brought low, fears its self-created isolation and screams in the wilderness of its own searching and suffering, not knowing that obstacles exist solely to be overcome. That sickness and suffering arise from within and are not enemies without, is not yet an idea which has taken root in the fragile heart of Everyman. It was in this way that an organization great in objectives and intentions began to crumble as individual failings gnawed at its structures and weakened the minds which held it together as they repeated the unlearned lessons of history.

There are three weapons we can use – science, philosophy and morality, the first appealing to the material, the second to the mental and the third to the spiritual parts of humankind. Many times quarrelling has broken out as to which should be used and jealousies have grown over the skilfulness and dexterity of the wielders, for if one emerges with greater prowess, others less able, fear and imagine their own to be an enemy. You could not understand that the human is prey to an instability by which he imagines that the superior ability of another diminishes his own. It is in such ways that doors are left ajar and the dark ones set foot inside. Then inch by inch they creep, invisibly, to do their black works.

There are some who may recognize the presence of these shadowy entities, but for them, the fight against them is hardest of all. Unseen, they have insinuated themselves and those that see are not believed, but that their source is the same as that which has possessed the enemy, is certain.

Such is the web which evil weaves among us, from which your kind is free, but a victim.

Such jealousies had grown and science, so tainted with its idolatrous worship by our enemy, lies under dark suspicion and this very mistrust in our revolutionaries breeds thoughts which lead to self-inflicted wounds.

Wounds that take long to heal. And that is why I write your story, Dear Dog.

Restless and weary, haunted by the faces of those left behind, I wait for you. Here, with this pledge to you, I leave these pages. Conjuring once more the image of your face so full of trust, I do solemnly promise to work this thing through.

Chapter 9

It was a noisy evening. People were there to dinner, filling the house with their chatter. Frances finds their talk to be mostly of superficial things. They believe they can put the world right with politics – a crude tool which only scratches the surface of our problems. They speak of 'the State' as if it were a machine to bring everything to order to the benefit of all, forgetting that we, with all our varied and demanding individuality, are an integral part of that unyielding amorphous body. Neither politics nor enterprise will make us more generous or stop us poisoning the Earth which gave us life. It is hard for us to stare too long, if at all, into the deeps of our own subconscious minds.

One poor young woman, who declared herself a Christian, argued that science had been bestowed upon us by a gracious God and should it postulate some potential gain for mankind, then creatures are ours to sacrifice upon its altars. Frances falls into her conversation when she hears her support abhorrent research with genuine enthusiasm. When she tells her that Jesushood means the 'All compassionate', that one in such a state can have no part in harm, anger draws all the blood from her drawn face until she feels the very knife in her own hand. When she tells her that to sacrifice is to make sacred, to uphold, nourish and beautify, the very antithesis of robbing of life, she freezes as if Frances had given her a mortal blow. Frances fears this woman would smile, praying heavenward, all decked in a long, brown habit, as martyrs scorch in agony in a holy fire!

The truth can shatter. We are outnumbered, but we are one with the stars and we shall travel fearless through 'His vasty Night'.

She had read about a great teacher dog who taught his human to look. He took his man on long walks and showed him how to contemplate the farthest horizon, tuning into the vibrations of the earth and sky where body and soul meet. She had learnt this same meditation from a human and was not surprised to learn a dog could teach it. She believes the dog taught it better, his thought patterns uncluttered.

She feels very cluttered with her guests' aggressive organizing talk, and seeks relief walking outside into the garden in the darkness. To find a stillness. To reconcile. To clear. Away from them, she could reach their invisible hidden parts which they could not dare to reveal in the company of others. She can feel her own thoughts stretching out into the night.

Through the trees, along the lawns, up and down the terraces, she walks, with slow, determined steps, hoping for something. There is hardly any moonlight. Suddenly, she feels cut off. Forsaken. Lost. She chants a poet's words for comfort, scattering them upon the night air, hoping they might prove a benison for those of us who care:

> *Truth crushed to earth, will rise again,*
> *The eternal years of God are hers,*
> *But error, wounded, writhes in pain,*
> *And dies among his worshippers.*

She speaks aloud to the stars: 'May truth sustain us through the Darkness. Please do not ever leave me, dear spirits of the Dogs. We are placed to live in time, but let's try to live as if we were not of Time, but of the Eternal. You and I, together. I know I am very demanding, but we will work this thing through.'

She wakes next morning to pouring rain, battering the windows, dripping from the trees, the ground harbouring trapped pools of water growing larger by the minute. As she comes into consciousness, she feels she has vaguely seen the Black Dog, but he is asleep. She could not reach him. Although she longs to talk with him, she's glad to wake.

Everyone grumbling, the boys want to be outside, Joe's mood is dampened, the day is so heavy with the rain. The greyness of the sky hems in their spirits. Sometimes she enjoys the rain. Perhaps because it shuts her into herself and gives dreaming space. She had had to rush and write this dream memory before the movement of the day began because the dog and perhaps Franziska were somehow there. The image had to be captured on to the page, however fleeting.

She goes walking with the boys and the dogs through the woods, taking the longest tracks. She needs time to think. The rain continues and as it beats on their faces, she wonders if Black Dog enjoyed rain, if wet-nosed and bright-eyed he would splash carelessly through the puddles with the boys, and if, like her dogs, he would wade muddied to the hocks through the bushes and come running, tail wagging, to be stroked, with pieces of spring flower pollen and small fallen petals stuck to his damp face, to share the happiness? The strong smell of moist fur follows her into the room. He is everywhere.

He and the creature kingdom are owed an explanation.

Back at the house, Joe, having finished writing a melody he's pleased with, makes the boys cheery cocoa. They are energised by the walk. Frances happily joins them before going to her room to lay more pressing thoughts upon the waiting pages. She leaves their sons helping Joe to prepare their lunch.

A new day of awareness is beginning to dawn; after the hundred years' war in which your and my enemies have gained in power and prestige and during a time in which those fighting them had been weakened and rendered largely ineffectual, things have begun to change. A new generation has arisen with fire in their hearts which their forebears lacked. Many of them, not chained by the attachment to material security or the search for quiet niches of approbation in a hostile world so unforgiving to those who do not fit the images of others' likenesses. Wrought in desolation, we have become the conscience of our society.

Its weakened will is being put through the purging fire. It is they who will break the spell and by their refusal to take part in the magic potions of a poisoned science, the blood of your kind will be washed from the hands of a race deformed by ignorance of our Oneness.

The newly awakened ones took burning torches and lit a brighter light. The noise of victory to come was loud in their ears. But there was a fatal flaw of which they were oblivious. They were not all without some of the darkness in their hearts and sometimes danced to the tune of forces who would mislead them and keep your cages locked.

Even they too could not bear to look too far into the deep waters of their subconscious. Despising leaders, they could not help but produce them.

You would understand about leaders. The strong dog would take responsibility for his pack and not lead them into danger or abandon them when needed.

Your kind could teach our kind a thing or two about the fierceness of loyalty. Our human race considers itself rather too superior instead of a part of the whole and a steward of the weaker parts. It is only the few gifted with a special kind of sight who learn from your kind.

Most people seem to imagine that a dog is a dog, and a human is a human and that a great gulf divides them. They persist in the illusion of separation, they are lonely and, in their loneliness, anger thrashes wildly inward and then erupting, lashes out. The irony is, that it is because of our loneliness that we make you suffer. If we embraced you, if we crossed the gulf, it would melt away the need for the magic to cure the disease. The disease would be gone.

That would be a true healing. Soon you and I shall show how that is so.

I did not dream of you at all last night, perhaps because I wanted to so much. Instead, I was caught in knots of sleeplessness, in which convoluted tangles of mental processes closed the door to oblivion.

Anger still lives inside me. Some mockery of a professor who mutilates cats was given a great deal of space on the airwaves this morning, and looking at my own cats lining up for their breakfast, I could not help but think for a passing minute that fate might turn against him for his wickedness or that all the cats in the world might scratch at his dark eyes for all their kittens he had blinded in the name of curiosity which, he has stated in private, 'can have no possible clinical application'. But revenge is simply the victim partaking in the crime. A respectable member of the great English middle-classes, with a wife, three children and a dog, he will smile at old ladies in his smart suburb. His students say he's charming.

The charm of the devil, I think, living off *their* blindness. But we, being imperfect, are part of his crime.

How hard this is to live with; almost as if living were dying, it brings me to the very edge of existence.

Our mutual Creator will judge him or, if he has a soul, it will lead him to the consequences of his actions until he sees another way.

So much patience is required of us, but you are teaching me. You lead, and I follow.

Chapter 10

The children's voices, shouting and excited, spread through the house, mixed with the warm smell of toast which Joe is making for tea. The 4.30 teatime is a ritual as necessary to him as a call to prayer. It brings him back and mingles him with the schoolboys returned. Frances hears them kicking a football around in the hall. These homely noises jolt her out of her attunement with something other.

Her study door swings open and bangs against the wall. She startles and turns. 'Mum, the horses are on the steps again – they want to get in the door.'

Frances gets up, smiling. 'They can smell the toast. Why don't you give them some? Why don't we let them in?'

'They're too big, and they'd ruin the floor.'

'Oh wuh . . .'

The small boy runs off down the corridor and Frances follows.

Joe will have a neat pile of his home-made bread toasted, sitting ready on the long kitchen table. He's calling the boys.

'Hello mummy,' he'll joke, when she follows them into the kitchen. He needs more than the mother inside him, she thinks. His own was a hard surface, unyielding in her self-centredness. The only tears she felt were her own, welling up from a pool of self-pity or sentimental indulgence. They want her to join them eating warm toast dripping with honey from Joe's bees. She'll be there. She walks across the wide hallway, abandoned for the kitchen now, and going to the large main door, opens it. There on the wide shallow steps, is the grey mare. Frances nuzzles against her huge face, breathes in her horse smell and takes strength from her. The horse's eyes half close, dreamily, as she rubs behind her ears. The horse is easy company, as she breathes deeply against the falling of the light, leaning gently against this mass of a creature who has no idea of its strength and stands perfectly, reassuringly still, an unconditional creaturely body of comfort.

No idea of their own strength, no conception of it, she thinks again to herself as she turns to make for the kitchen, reluctant to shut her horse out. Sometimes I feel as if I could stride the world and sometimes, I'm in the smallest locked cage, unable to move, its bars just like the rope we string across a gap in the fence to stop the horses escaping. It bars their way, but in reality, it may as well be a thread unwound from a cobweb. And that web, spun with blind assurance can be whisked away in a moment by the unknown finger, the stranger passing...

'Where are you?' a young voice shouts. Jack thumps up the stairs from the basement, takes hold of her and pulls her back down with him to family teatime. Joe has already planned dinner. Frances wants to run outside. She often fears the fading of the daylight, but then there is always a longing she feels when she looks at the stars. Such a deep mystery is that vastness.

She is always relieved when the sun slowly breaks through night's darkness, painting out the stars.

Frances likes best of all to be out there with the birds, to be part of dawn.

The chatter in the kitchen is comforting in its normality. It brings her back to the everyday. The boys never fail to surprise her with their fresh, insightful observations. She offers to help with French homework and Joe presses for piano practice, silencing protest with praise for their talent. 'You'd be sorry forever if you wasted it,' he says, his face serious with conviction as a dog nudges his elbow for a titbit.

'I really regret not carrying on with mine,' Frances joins in. 'Now I'm frustrated I can hardly play a thing and I've no time to practise.'

'You prefer to rescue animals,' Jack says, pulling his schoolwork out of his bag.

She smiles and thinks of the dog. She'll write to him again later, out of a deep need to explain everything to herself and to feel she is somehow communicating with him.

Later, Frances is pulled back to her room, not by the black dog, but by Franziska tugging at her sleeve, saying, 'It is not yet finished, their work – the work the Nazis wrought upon the world. Do you think what they left can pass so quickly? Listen to us, the Ghosts of Time and we will show you...'

May, 1933
Something terrible is occurring. Our culture is being destroyed. Yesterday evening piles of wonderful books by German and foreign authors were burnt in the streets and students joined in with the burning. I cannot believe that they would do this. It is an intellectual *auto-da-fé* and belongs to medieval times. Any books that are considered 'subversive' to our future were condemned to the bonfire. We are sliding backwards into a terrible Dark Age.

Joseph Goebbels addressed the students as the books burned, telling them that, 'The soul of the German people can again express itself.' He declared it was the end of an old era and the 'illumination of the new'. Germany is losing its soul.

A torchlight parade at midnight ended opposite the university. I watched with a friend in horror, tears in my eyes. Our country is so sick, I am afraid it will die of the poison it is so willingly swallowing. It is deadly.

When the students and the SA carried the books so gleefully into the fire, it felt like the end of civilization. Now we can face only barbarism.

June, 1933
We are all supposed to join the BDM (League of German Girls). It is

the girls' version of the Hitler Youth and I cannot bear it. They are hysterical fanatics and I try to stay aloof, but I don't want their attention. What is more, we are supposed to do the Heil Hitler salute at the beginning and end of every lesson. Fraulein Niemeier is really keen on it. I am very half-hearted and sometimes pretend I have injured my arm. She whacked me with a ruler when she thought I was refusing one day.

There have been rallies of Hitler Youth. They are boys playing at soldiers, worshipping the Fuhrer, shouting *Heil!* It is tragic and I pity them. This devil-worship will turn back on them one day. It feels as if there is a battle being fought for our very souls.

I know it is very dangerous for me to write this diary and to keep it, but I feel I must. I must bear witness. We are living through a most evil time in history. Papa and Bertie agree with me on that. They believe Hitler will start a war and then the flames of hell will engulf us and, who knows, the world?

July, 1933
We are losing even more freedoms. In March Hitler took away our parliamentary democracy. He is now a dictator. The huge claws of the German eagle has us in its cruel grip. Shall we ever escape?

July, 1933
I was in the public library this afternoon. I like to study, but I do not know if I shall get into a university now, as places for girls have been reduced to just ten per cent while the boys get ninety per cent. I was quietly reading and making notes. I am studying English and was engrossed in the world of the book, a history of England written in English, so that I had to concentrate on every word. I kept a dictionary beside me.

Suddenly there was a great disturbance, a banging and crashing and shouting. The librarian at her desk looked up over her spectacles as the doors swung open and several SA crashed into our silent sanctuary. One of them marched up to the desk and spoke to her male colleague, a man perhaps in his forties sorting books, and told him what to say. Obviously shocked, as these librarians tend to be quiet, rather studious people, he spoke out as best he could.

'Would all Jewish people kindly leave now.'

The Brownshirt turned round as a few people stood up and packed their books away.

The SA man grinned, showing his ugly yellow teeth. 'You have permission to leave, but make it quick – schnell!' They seemed flustered and some bungled the putting of papers into their bags.

I remained still as if frozen, looking at them. Then, I purposely carried on reading. This little group of brown bullies stood and watched with satisfaction at the leave-taking. I barely looked up, just glanced up for a moment and returned to the page, but the letters seemed to slide past my mind as if on ice. A minute later, a hand slapped on the page and a man's face thrust towards mine with its yellow teeth and bad dragon breath.

'*Bist Du Aryan?*' Are you Aryan?

'But of course!' I answered with a steady, firm voice and smiled, just a faint smile. At that moment, a streak of sunlight shone through the window above and fell upon my hand and the SA man's eyes glowed red.

'All right then,' the oaf answered and moved on to a young man whose hair was dark and snatched his book. I sat still and waited until they had finished and departed. Thankfully, they had demanded no identification. I was saved, but inside, I was trembling and it was hard to make myself stay there for another half an hour at that table. I wanted to make sure they had really gone away. I was hardly breathing.

I hurried home, needing to tell Papa what had happened. I thought

I had passed my first real test. He arrived back soon after me. I was still trembling when I told him. He put his arms around me, told me he was proud of my stand but that I should not take any more risks. It was far too dangerous.

'I had no idea of how lethal and ruthless the State Police are should I ever fall into their hands,' he said.

I do not think I shall have fun young years. I see another future for myself, but if I must die, I will return again from the ashes. We are all walking with our destinies.

Frances feels she walks with hers with her present preoccupations. It is not an easy path to follow.

Chapter 11

I wrote to you about human leaders. There are two types, those who set themselves up because they want glory and those who cannot help but lead in spite of themselves because they have a natural strength which magnetizes others. There are natural leaders among your kind too, but not unnatural ones. I know this would be too hard for you to understand, but I am finding my way through an intricate maze in writing to you. I know you are an innocent and made of love. It is that which allows me to address this to you.

Unnatural leaders had risen to a certain standing at the time of our first troubles.

Growing unchecked, negative thought patterns began to strangle those who harboured them and like poison ivy, harmed all those who touched them unaware.

All this happened among those who were fighting to liberate your kind from those among our kind who were your oppressors.

The struggle appears endless; it stretches before us like a sea of horrors, far into the horizon. And the sea is blood red.

Sometimes, despairing at the enormity of their task, people turn upon their own. Their anger, frustrated in its course and failing to reach the real enemy, turns upon a nearer, easier target, because it has been forcibly pushed back.

Maybe you understand that, for all of us from the mammal kingdom know about the outward projection of aggression in enforced confinement upon those who would normally either be friends or go unnoticed. This happened in their minds and they could not control it, because their anger was constantly being rendered ineffectual by the greater evils which presently rule our world.

I hope then, that by seeing our way through this, we can help each other out of the twilight of doubt.

The quiet fighting continued and negativity was insidiously directed at one of the strongest of your defenders. This quiet, silent, strangling growth hid itself meanwhile in routine disagreements over the methods and approach to the problems we all had to solve. The problems were immeasurably great, but fell into categories too clearly in minds made up as to which way was best or would win first or most. We have the mind of the nation to convince, and the very mind of the world. The Law on experimentation on animals was going to be changed. Our group wanted abolition, no less. The others were very willing to compromise.

Nominations for our committee were put forward which were surprising to some of us, but we were outnumbered by those who supported them.

One newcomer, so obviously ambitious for himself, but who could make a mark in no other way upon a world which loves status, stormed in, hair shaven, dressed in camouflage clothes and heavy boots. It was difficult to find any love in him. He trod upon feelings – he could not articulate his own – and ignored the office dogs who ran among the desks or lay on our feet to sleep. He only wanted to hear his voice or see his own face with its staring eyes look out from a television screen.

There were times when emotion overtook Brigitte, our fiery-haired 50-year-old Irish woman, who spoke in quiet, quick, lilting tones. Her voice would sometimes be raised to screaming in the heat of discussions where everyone heard, but no one listened. And then the door would slam behind her, signifying her defeat. Broken spirited, she returned to her small flat-full of strays and looked for consolation in their devoted, undemanding company. She wasn't made for committees and this one took her into waters where she almost drowned.

Others looked for respectability and were afraid to live alongside liberationists whose stories they proclaimed, enjoying a kind of reflected glory while in reality maintaining a safe distance. Seeing their success and the attention given to those soldiers in the front line, made others feel that they were dangerous and violent and that they must be rooted out, set apart. This protest came from unexpected sources: it was those without particular skills, learning, income or worldly standing who reached for bureaucracy and locked the rescuers out from the growing comfort of their office premises. They wanted status and protection from the risky stain of radicalism.

A blonde-haired girl with fluttering eyes and her lorry driver boyfriend with a bunch of keys hanging from his belt pushed the most sensible intelligent, honest and useful employee Pamela, out of the office. Others, who understood the plot too late, allowed her, undefended, to go. A terrible injustice and your most articulate defender was silenced.

The office manager, whose personality had become deformed by a sense of power, listened to no one and began to lose his hair, along with his compassion.

Pat, the dark-haired boyfriend of the fluttering blonde, had wild eyes which flamed in tempers fit to kill and promised dark things to any who disagreed. Gone were the smiles, the warmth, the enthusiasms of earlier days. A collective madness held sway and bound us to a sadness we could not understand.

It was as if former goodness had been swallowed in the eye of the storm which raged continually around the building. Conversations were recorded for the purposes of condemnation; past mistakes dredged up like rotting carcasses and put on show.

Those who felt wronged became scornful, hurt, sick. The fluttering blonde spat her hatreds out, set her lips firm and by pure determination achieved her desires. She worked hard in a masochistic way, day in and day out. There was a kind of caring, but like the sun on a day of uncertain weather, it was all too often obscured.

Why do they forget your pleading helplessness, Dear Dog? Many of us hurt because we feel your pain of rejection: the impenetrable eyes walled in the human head, love suffocated and dying inside. This dying, this killing of all that means life is the evil we have to fight. In a world without animals, man will not survive. The mystery of the life of your kind is hidden from them, yet somehow the unconscious guilt is taking them towards self-destruction entangled as they are in feelings they cannot understand. We are all joined by the golden web of life and cannot escape.

I know all these things, and yet, my life is not free from the illusions all humans suffer and every time I am caught up in anger where there should be understanding, I know I have fallen prey to the illusion of self as separate from the Whole.

We move amidst this collective delusion, sometimes glimpsing the Truth, but only momentarily.

Some approach the problem directly and physically remove animals from the cages of science. By freeing you, we are beginning the freeing of ourselves.

Man, because he cannot at present live intuitively, by natural law, as your kind can, makes laws by which to order his society. The laws evolve slowly with the consciousness of the people. As yet, man has very little conscience about the way he treats other species, and does little to protect them by Law.

It seems as if the threat lies in their innocence, for, guilty in a thousand ways, he cannot carry the burden.

There are always prisoners of war, held captive and tortured at times of fighting between man and man. There are prisoners of war held captive and tortured permanently in this time of fighting between man and his darker self.

As in all wars, the pacifists are crushed, because our calls in the wilderness of evil sound like madness to the masses mesmerized by the evil that exists as a current reality. That which is different cannot be readily understood. That which is different is therefore mocked. That which is different causes fear in the masses who look for outward security in the sameness of an existence which they cannot understand as an illusion. The violent man is an inferior man. He cannot bear that we should name him.

Those who, in their ignorance, hang on to the coat-tails and ingest the propaganda of your captors imagine that the animals owe this sacrifice to them. Those among men and women who feel they are owed something suffer from a feeling of inferiority, and this, in its turn, makes them angry. And they do not know it. Such people can never stand alone yet they are isolated by their fear.

Most of our kind suffer from our dark shadow which we hide away as if it did not, could not, exist. The shadow controls and we blame in others those things of which we ourselves are guilty, yet if we could but name them in ourselves, we would transform them into wisdom precious as pearls.

Frances glances at the time. It is late – too deep into night's dark hours and the night is heavy with cloud – no stars to light it. She knows Joe will already be sleeping and tiptoeing to her sons' rooms, she kisses their sleeping faces and thinks how Franziska's mother must have often done the same after returning from the theatre and wonders how sad and empty she must have felt when in England there was no daughter to kiss and how she must have surely cried herself to sleep. Frances goes to bed, gives thanks for its comfort and feeling overwhelming gratitude for her sons, also feels tears falling on to the white linen of her pillow for all the captive dogs and for Dear Dog who stands for them all as her soul, released by sleep, flies to them.

Next morning, as soon as the house is quiet, she goes back to him.

*

Dear Dog, I see you so clearly in my mind that it is as if we are together. The reality of thought is so often counted for little in our world, yet in thought we touch others who are thousands of miles away. Because you came to know me in those minutes out of time, I believe you have received my thoughts, and understanding, have taken some comfort. I hope I shall not fall short of my promises to you. I have told the other dogs about you. They listened attentively, for several moments, their eyes fixed on mine, then, as if they had registered the message, whined, responding with eagerness. I count you among them, here to receive all the affection you might want or need: A way for us to be able to express the love which needs to flow and help ease the sorrows of the world.

One day, we must all stand alone and suffer inasmuch as we have caused suffering. But we are never allowed to judge. That is not for us in all our imperfection. That is hardest of all for me, when I consider your tormentors and betrayers. We cannot see clearly, just as I cannot see you as I would dearly wish, but perhaps you will help to erase the hatred from my scarred heart. That is why I'm writing this, to serve you, to attempt to turn a torment into a blessing. I know, but cannot reach that place. Understanding is the way of strength. As you trusted, so I must trust you in my groping, searching out the path to the truth.

As the seed rests silently in the dark earth and awaits its awakening, so do I wait in my own cloud of unknowing, assured that the sun and the rain of the spirit will somehow perform their alchemy and bring forth a newness into the light of day.

Frances reluctantly closes her notebook, returning it to her secret cupboard, letting him rest between its covers and turns to her research. Books are waiting to be read to fill in details of Franziska's life and she owes it to her not to ignore them any longer.

*

I dozed while reading this afternoon and had an exciting dream. I dreamt that my house was vast, but that there were many hidden and neglected rooms which I longed to explore. They are not here in reality. There are no secret rooms among these bricks, and yet I awoke knowing that I had wonderful discoveries to make, but also knowing that there was one door locked to me – and I could not find the key. I know that the house is me and the dream seemed to be some sort of a reward for reaching out. Dare I give myself such a prize? Will it make it go away? Only one thing spoiled the thrilling atmosphere: as I tried that handle of the locked door, I somehow felt as if your shadow, not you, much larger than life, fell across me in the dusky light.

I had fallen asleep because I wanted to escape. I don't think even those closest to me understand the hell I've been through. My husband says I should get on with living, not mope, complain, not dip constantly into what is past. He doesn't understand our very necessary journey, Dear Dog. But I believe that you and I are moving onwards in our own way. Because he cannot understand these thoughts, instead of ignoring his opinion, I demand understanding and become upset. But tears only choke the flow of knowing. It is self-pity and it hinders me. Then I think of your life and pull myself back from the greyness and reach again towards the light.

We had a good, expanding organization which made excellent propaganda on behalf of animals used in experiments. Some spoke with knowledge and passion on your behalf. Posters with shocking pictures and words which appealed to compassion were everywhere, illegally stuck on any available space. From these, animals called out their pain. A great many people joined together in large demonstrations. A new spirit of youthful enthusiasm had infected our cause. The old, polite and lumbering ways were gone for good.

A vital movement seemed to speak with a pure, new voice and it had the ring of victory.

Despite the once formidable and immovable opposition, there was a certainty in the air. Righteous anger poured on to the radio waves and reached the television screens. The voice was so good and strong that the lies of the enemy were being revealed. A new consciousness began to rise; and so slowly and in small part, sleeping consciences, informed, were being awoken.

A new day was dawning.

But then came a feeling of power in those who before had never known it and a worm ate slowly away at the fabric of our organization which had proclaimed itself a true democracy, for humans and animals as one. Somehow, tragically, the animals fell into second place.

In the great books which humans read, looking for direction as to how they should live, the story is told of a Holy Teacher who was persecuted and killed because the people feared his truth. It was a betrayal by one of his followers who, in an hour of weakness, fell under the spell of the dark shadow which hovers over mankind, which opened the door to the murderers. His name was Judas. But his was but a mistake. There was a greater betrayer – a power of Darkness as old as the Fall. Later this man murdered himself, as the spell fell away, as remorse rose up and choked him to death, that he had been so used. His part was in an earthly event, but there was tragedy far greater than this.

The true betrayer remained hidden and realized his dark vision, unbeknown even to those who believed they followed the Great Teachings which so soon were taken and their purity subtly changed. So it came to be that by the crucifixion of what He taught, your kind are still persecuted and wolves, wearing the masks of lambs, walk unnoticed in every street.

We began to feel that somewhere, there was a betrayer among us, used by invisible powers, helping to betray the Light. The powers of darkness are always at work.

He or she – for darkness also lives in the mostly gentler nature of womankind – was either one we knew well or moved silently among those who worked closest to the heart of the organization, feeding their fears, nourishing the lower sense of selfhood which desires imagined power and influence and imagines that the strength of the shouting bully is real. Whether it was one person or an energy emanating from our enemies – your oppressors – we could not tell, and blindly, we were bound to resist its increasing power.

Our energies, unprotected, drained easily. In the endless hours of dispute, we fought against a wall of ignorance as people whirled towards two poles, perceiving in the most normal words or actions, dark motives which lived in the shadows cast by the figures of their egos, each standing isolated upon its own patch, stubborn, wilful. Enthralled by their own echoes, there were those who were deaf to other voices, so that good things died in the air before they could find a resonance.

The negativity from within allowed the negativity from without to enter and rule. As the way was made and its dwelling place came to be, so did the light of hope dim for those of your kind who waited behind the bars of locked laboratory cages.

At times, when the clouds of irritation, intolerance and rage blew into the room, we forgot our true selves and instead of being shielded from their oppression by making our own lights bright, we often allowed them to engulf us. Our perceptions were closed to the inner voice and our judgement mingled with the cloud and became lost to us.

And so the quarrels grew like a mould in an atmosphere which denied the cleansing light of the sun. Friend turned against friend, as seeing their own failings reflected in others, none could escape the poisoned circle.

Some of us saw this time coming long before it took its place in our reality, but we had neither strength nor guile enough to turn it away, and more than this, we were but a few.

It is said that even the Great One found it hard or impossible, at times, to do his good works, so enormous was the weight of negativity from the people about him, so what hope for us who know so little? So Dear Dog, you and I shall hold these words up to the Light and let the Light do its work. I am asking for your co-operation. It is impossible to leave you alone.

The words shall be faithful copies, the feelings, lived through yet again and perhaps, in the sharing, we shall find a solution. I carry you now, a welcome weight, upon my shoulders. For it is said that if we save a life, we are responsible for it until its end.

In the quiet of my study, where the page stands between us, in the stillness of my aloneness, and especially in the peace of the night when thinking is put away, you are there.

When I leave you for the business of the everyday, of people, voices and objects which demand, I feel I have forsaken a friend and later guilt jibes at me, for although the space we share is infinite, perhaps there are some things which cannot wait. Together, I think we are attempting to attain the Holy Instant. Your power of attainment is something which cannot yet be understood.

For it is that no meeting of any note happens by chance, and all the blindness in the world cannot alter the pattern as created.

In the morning, as the sun lights up the world in dawn's pink glow, so shall I bring those pages into that light and the pink light of the Creator's renewed love of the earth shall be a seal upon them and with the new dawn, they shall be enlightened.

Frances has lost a large part of her day. It is already afternoon. The morning rushed by with too many distractions. Her husband left at nine, agitated and bad-tempered because he was late for an appointment. He was in no mood to sense her feelings of hurt and isolation which yearned for a simple note of sympathy. Perhaps she had become lost in this dream. He constantly talks to her of realism, but when he does stop to listen, he listens to the dreams which sometimes become his own. Then they change their shape, but not their substance.

The boys demanded small things of her – they lost their sports gear, forgot the appointment with the dentist, arrived late for piano lessons, needed more cash and then asked her why she wasn't working at her desk when tears of frustration began to show. Perhaps they feared for the paths she trod and snatched her back in little and unwilling ways.

Meanwhile, the dogs followed them around, sat when they sat, bounded up and down the stairs with them, barking with an unfathomable excitement whenever they approached a door to go outside. They are all in their pack. Their day after day sameness is a joy to her. Such a natural rhythm rules their lives.

She sees how no one is ever more important to them than those they have chosen to join up with and love.

She snatches a quiet hour and hopes there was no fear for the black dog. Dogs live in the moment. But his moment is safe for now. She knows that it is reaching back and beyond that stretches our pieces of happiness to breaking.

Chapter 12

Early afternoon and quiet. Dot, the help, is ironing on the lower ground floor. Frances is in her study, writing. Far into her own world. Joe arrived home earlier than expected from his morning appointment and has gone straight to work in his studio.

Frances, completely absorbed, is jolted into shock at the loud, insistent banging on the front door as if it were a dawn raid. The dogs are barking wildly. Her window is open. She goes to look below. Dot had gone to open the door. On the wide stone steps are two uniformed police constables. Frances feels alarm. They might question her. She must be prepared. Losing her cool for a moment because policemen always seem to her to have a menacing air when they think they might be on to something; she stops and takes three deep breaths.

First, she hurriedly ties and closes the notebook in which she had been writing with trembling hands to the black dog. She slips it into her underwear, glad she is wearing a loose dress. She might have to change this she thinks quickly, should they try and take her in for questioning. No, that wouldn't happen, she is sure of it. This isn't the Gestapo. She isn't Franziska. She then gathers up some ALF news sheets and a few of the more radical animal rights books lying around. She slips off her shoes and opening her study door very quietly, tiptoes along the corridor to their bedroom where she goes to the door into the hidden cupboard she had had made when they bought this house. It is disguised as a bookcase and no one who didn't know could tell. She had always wanted a secret cupboard and now it felt very much like prescience. Hiding the books and papers and the notebook under a pile of antique textiles her merchant navy uncle had brought back from the Far East, she steps back out and slips the hidden lock, making sure it looks just like the undisturbed bookcase it is.

Walking very quietly back to her room, she feels a threatening wave of fear in her legs and knows then how Franziska must have felt – but she had been in far more serious danger. These two were not the Gestapo, but for the animals, they were. Innocents taken into imprisonment and torture. She is thankful her car is in the garage for servicing and it is a courtesy car they have lent her which sits in the driveway beside Joe's blue Renault estate. She makes her way silently to the bannister at the top of the stairs where she can listen, hidden, to what is going on. Dot, who belongs to the local pot-smoking culture and has a healthy suspicion of the police, has gone to fetch Joe in his studio to the right of the main door. He obviously hasn't rushed out.

'Two coppers at the door, Joe,' Dot says loudly in her Hereford accent. 'Has someone died, Dot?' he asks with a smile.

'I dunnow,' she says, 'I'm glad it's not me they're after, leastways.'

Joe smiles, seals the envelope to the letter he'd been writing, addresses it and leaves it on his desk, then goes to see what they want. The dogs are still barking as he steps out and asks, 'Good afternoon, officers, how can I help you?'

They step inside, uninvited. Joe notes how they look a little surprised at the space, the large square wood-panelled entrance hall with its giant log fireplace and watches them briefly cast their eyes over his full-size Bechstein grand piano. Frances remembers how hard they'd worked to restore this house which had twice been used as a school in the last thirty years. She had fallen in love with it at first sight despite its then scruffy appearance.

'We'll just take a look around if you don't mind.' Joe frowns. 'Well, I might –'

Frances is glad the boys aren't home to be questioned. They have choir practice after school today and will be late.

'Reports of a dog –' Number One copper, the pushier of the two, replies. The one who believes he's the lead man.

Joe frowns again. The dogs, quiet now, gather round him.

'Who are these, then?' Number One enquires, indicating the gang of dogs.

'Lolita,' Joe points to a small Spanish terrier, 'Sir Walter, aka Wally,' pointing to the rough-haired mongrel terrier, 'Matilda,' who is a soft-natured golden retriever, 'Mr Collins,' an Irish collie, 'and this fellow here, is Lord Cecil Llewellyn, named after a distant late cousin who loved large dogs,' he says fondling the head of the large grey deerhound.

The two policemen look at each other with raised eyebrows. 'They are all rescues,' Joe states with some pride in his voice.

'Are they indeed?' Number One starts to fiddle with Lord Cecil's ears. The dog growls. 'What are you doing?' Joe asks.

'Tattoos,' pushy Number One says.

'What's this all about?' Joe asks in all innocence as Number One moves to the next dog and the next, but Lolita wriggles from his grasp.

'Identification, sir – of stolen property.'

'These are our pets – or companion animals, as we prefer to call them.'

'You don't mind if we take a look in your office.' They walk towards it, uninvited. Joe shrugs. 'Perhaps I do. Can I see your warrant?'

'If you've nothing to hide, sir –'

Number One sees the addressed letter on the desk and fingers it. 'The Hon. Mr Justice Dobbs. A friend of yours, is he? Bit of a maverick, that one.'

Joe fights the irritation at their poking around and their over-familiar talk. 'Yes, he is a good friend and a fan of my work.'

'What's that, then, sir?'

'I'm a composer – mostly film music.' There is a poster for *Storm over the Wilderness* on the wall.

'Did you write that music?' Copper Number Two finally speaks.

'It's great.' he is grinning. 'There's a clever man you are,' he says in his Welsh accent. 'There's some great songs in it and all.'

Copper Number One looks at him with a tight smile, perhaps displeased at the distraction from the task he feels he has in hand.

'You must have seen it, Bri, it's really popular, it is.' He seems excited by his discovery.

'Indeed, Wayne, I have,' Bri replies, casting his eyes around Joe's technical equipment. 'I hope you've got decent insurance for this lot.'

Joe merely shakes his head in disbelief. Policemen are always expecting crime, he thinks, whereas he is expecting no such thing.

'Shall we proceed, then?'

Frances, hearing this, quickly goes back to her room and sits at her desk, trying to concentrate. She summons all the cool she can muster, inwardly furious.

A few moments later, there are heavy footsteps on the stairs and the opening and shutting of doors along the corridor. Joe walks in front of the two intruders, followed by the five dogs. He knocks on her door, with, 'Darling, we have two officers here who want to "take a look around".'

'What on earth for?' Frances asks.

'Possible stolen property, madam, namely dogs. I understand your dogs are all rescued,' suggesting there could be a problem.

'Of course they are, we'd never buy our animals from breeders. One of them is from my own charity which rescues strays in Greece.'

'I see.' He starts poking around, notes her typewriter and various papers and notes lying around. There are one or two framed posters of her work on the walls.

'You a writer, then, are you madam?' 'Yes.' She hates their intrusive questions.

'I understand you're interested in animal rights.'

'I am. Human rights, as well. One of my books has discussed the important parallels.' Who are these horrible intruders? She feels indignant.

'And what would that book be called?'

'*Two Nations*.'

She goes up and pulls a copy from a line of them on her shelves. They glance at it, look along her bookshelves where they find nothing of particular interest.

'We'll just take a look in the other rooms, if you don't mind, sir,' Bri, the lead man says as he walks out into the corridor and proceeds to open doors without asking first. Joe turns and gives his wife a tight smile of exasperation as he turns back to follow them. Frances comes behind. They pass a Steve Bell drawing of the Home Secretary in a cage with a large monkey peering over him, but are too daft to take much notice. When they enter the main bedroom, they look around, open the wardrobe doors, notice only clothes and close them again, much to Joe's consternation, look closely at the books on the shelves. Bri stares at the bookcase for too long before pulling out a couple of books, one of them *Animal Farm*, the other a novel called *Uncaged*, which catches his eye, but puts them straight back again, with, 'Read a lot, do you?'

'Yes, a great deal. We both do.' She can see Joe is feeling even more irritated at these two nosey, unthinking men, but hides it behind a polite facade that is being so stretched. He hopes they'll just give up and leave.

'I like to read a good book, I do,' Wayne states as if pleased at his reading prowess. 'Thrillers is best.'

As they proceed back down the corridor, Wayne notices the drawing. 'Hey, look, Bri, that's good isn't it?'

Bri looks.

Joe says, 'It's by Steve Bell, The *Guardian* cartoonist. He's a friend of ours and drew it for one of my wife's campaigns during which we'd hope to change the Law for the better regarding experiments on animals, along with the help of our other friend, Linus Dobbs.'

'Likes animals, does he?' Bri asks as if he were equal to the High Court Judge.

'He does. He's very sympathetic and he's a vegetarian like us – or vegan now.'

'I don't know what you eat, do you, Wayne?'

Wayne grins.

'Lord Cecil Llewellyn is a vegetarian, as was his namesake,' Joe smiles. 'We are all very partial to vegetables, aren't we, old chap.'

'Never heard of a vegetarian dog,' Bri states. 'We all need a bit of protein.' Your pound of flesh, Frances thinks.

Finally, as if having run out of steam, these two seem to have had enough of searching.

They haven't quite given up, however, and noticing the stairs to the basement, proceed on down as if they've been invited. They pass large framed photographs of Oxbridge and schooldays on the wall down to the kitchen where the cupboards are plastered with photos of their animals and children.

'You've got kiddies, then,' Kev pronounces.

'Two sons.' Joe is now very tight-faced and Dot looks up and rolls her eyes, then frowns. 'You work here, then, do you?' Bri looks at Dot. He gives her a long, searching look. 'Yes,' is all she'll answer.

'Where do you live, then?'

'In the next village.' She looks sullen and resentful at this.

He looks at Dot, unnerving her slightly. 'I know your face from somewhere.' Dot shrugs.

'Thank you, sir. That'll be all for now,' Bri says as if he is leaving things open-ended as he reaches the door. Joe asks to see the warrant. 'Didn't need it, did we, sir.' Bri smiles. 'Thank you for your co-operation.'

Wayne is grinning inanely and can't resist putting his hand out to shake Joe's – he's a famous man, after all. He probably wanted to ask for his autograph, and maybe he'd come back with the CD one day and ask him to sign it.

They glance at the two cars on the drive before getting into their own and driving off. Joe shuts the door, noticing Frances going upstairs to her room.

Dot comes running up hearing the front door shut. 'Got rid of 'em, then. Good riddance. Lord Cecil didn't like 'em at all, he didn't. 'E was growling away there . . .'

'Well done, old chap.' Joe smiles at Lord Cecil Llewellyn and strokes his head. The dog leans against his leg in affection.

'Let's all have a cup of tea in the kitchen, Dot, and take a breather.'

Dot goes off to put the kettle on and Joe leaps up the stairs two at a time all the dogs following. He opens Frances's door. 'Phew, they've gone. They seemed like a couple of thickos to me.'

Frances smiles. 'Thank you for handling them so well. But why did you let them in?'

'I didn't,' he said sharply. 'They pushed in uninvited. If you carry on as you are, you'll have us all in clink –'

Joe waited.

'So what would you have done, just left the dogs to rot in there?'

'No – oh to hell with it all.' He swivels round, angry, that the police came, that Frances might land them in trouble, that the world can be so mean a place. 'Dot's making tea in the kitchen.' He starts away.

'I'm seething. What the hell was it all about?' she shouts after him.

'Stolen dogs, they said.'

This makes Frances follow him downstairs, more anxious and alarmed.

Joe stops at the top of the stairs to the basement and turns, 'Someone must have talked.'

There is tension in the kitchen. Joe is uncomfortable. Frances is uneasy. She wants to know who tipped the police off. They must have taken someone in for questioning. She is furious that they were careless, furious the law upholds suffering, furious that there are ignoramuses like those two constables willing to uphold it without a second thought. *'For the animals,'* she agrees with Bashevis Singer, *'We are all Nazis.'*

'That Brian one's a sneaky fella – he'll get you for anything he can.' Dot knows him and thinks he'll remember her name later.

'Well, there's nothing here for him,' Joe says getting up. 'Let's forget him for now and get on.'

The day wears on to midnight and Frances sits alone with music playing after the family has gone to bed. She didn't want to have to defend the gloom which too often loads these days. The dogs lie on the sofa and on the floor, still, but watching. The notes, in a minor key, evoke a sadness which rises up in her. Seeing this, Mr Collins, the little sheepdog, puts his paws up on her shoulders and licks her face, just as a human being might rush to comfort another, yet without any complication. His black and white hairs cling to the folds of her wine-purple dress. There seems to be a certain uncomprehending sorrow in his brown eyes, as if he sees the pointlessness of mankind's tears. He soon cheers as he runs into the garden with the others for a last quick dash before settling for the night.

Frances asks herself if she imagines, in the moonlight, as he turns and bounces playfully in a circle, a black shadow, about his size? There, alone...

She holds her breath. No, it is not imagining. This is a presence all the more real for its substantial otherness.

In a moment it has gone and she is left only with a question which the electric light in its harshness almost blots out. Heart thumping, she rushes to save it. She goes to write it down, for all experience might be called ephemeral. It is in the recording that it is captured for sharing.

These months of eternal hostility from her own side; the lies, distortions, body blows, have left a bedraggled heap seeking a healing.

She remembers an old lady she knew who had fought for animals in a foreign land where they were stoned and beaten unashamedly who once said to her, 'People like us are cursed.'

It is an unknowing which causes the strong to torment the weak. But in sleepless night hours, she knows her truth.

Something, somewhere deep inside her remains untouched.

Her conviction of immortality cannot in this moment be shaken.

Chapter 13

Today dawn was not an ethereal rose where earth conjoined with endless inviting sky. It is a nubiferous hollow and Frances knows she must reach above the clouds which wouldn't allow the sun to blaze its arrival in glory, but cloak the light in damp silver-blue grey.

She thinks of the hundreds and thousands entering another day, who will go through its motions as if still inhabiting their confused dreams, who feel interminably helpless against all they innately abhor, as helpless as she has allowed herself to feel about the weather, a passivity she is grappling to overcome.

Joe observes this mood, but will not be drawn into it.

'Better finish the script. Your involvement beyond the call of duty is like a dangerous undertow which sucks you in.'

'Better to know, to know utterly.'

She is staring at the wall as if it were a screen presenting her with all of the pictures, she wishes to see in order to know. But the scene is jumbled. So much crowds in on her.

Joe makes the toast, puts a piece in front of her. Breakfast is conversation, setting up the day between them; a luxurious, consoling agreement denied the many who are enslaved to others' rules of time.

'Being involved is part of what I am.'

'But there is also what you might become. Those policemen had a damned cheek.'

Thankfully he has said little about the police invading their home and doesn't continue with blame and recrimination.

'It's the hardest of all, the hostility of those once called friends.'

Frances defends herself, but fears Joe's rejection of what he doesn't want in her. She knows she is languishing, battle-weary with not enough vitality left over for those who need a good part of her.

'We'll go away when I've finished this piece.' Her voice lightens momentarily and she takes a bite of the toast.

'Last night I dreamt of Franziska. She was sitting at my desk, smiling, but I couldn't talk to her . . . How many are too frightened, or too apathetic to follow their destiny? She was utterly sufficient unto herself, so unafraid.'

Frances is staring into the distance again. Freddie, the one-eyed cat, manages to pull the toast from her plate with a quick, deft movement and is crunching his prize contentedly at the other end of the table. Frances doesn't notice.

Joe is fascinated by such utter absorption with someone who is, to him, not real, but history, of only intellectual interest. He watches his wife change as though this young woman who disappeared over four decades ago were a pool into which she sinks daily, and emerging, looks other than she was before. The light and shadow paints her now in different colours as it comes and goes, filtering through the windows, not clouded, now streaked with tenuous light. He sees her shadowed and does not want lines to mourn on this familiar face, lines etched by a tragedy she has chosen.

'You are tangled with the wretched,' he protests. 'Like the weed in the river we've so often watched. That can be treacherous. The currents of life lived that way can be too swift and strong.'

Joe is frowning now as he talks. He knows she has gazed with horror into this dark, ancient river, become mesmerized. He wants to catch her, pull her back, pull her to the bank and safety.

'Can't you gaze from the bank, not risk yourself like this?' he asks.

'I don't know how. I have to know, to know it all, to feel what they feel, the wretched you talk of –' He wouldn't let her finish.

'Even the dead?'

'The dead don't live in time.'

'The new dog will soon be here.' Joe gets up, moves about, clearing plates away. He wants to break the atmosphere. Freddie is licking himself contentedly amidst a pile of damp crumbs. 'I hope that vet you lot have got removes tattoos without a trace. They mustn't have any evidence.'

'I feel him everywhere,' Frances says.

'Déjà vu,' Joe answers, hoping his concession to the possibility of stepping out of time will please her. 'Perhaps,' she smiles.

'To work. First things first.' Now he sounds a little like an army officer, but his only trooper at the ready and willing to obey is the small mongrel who trots at Joe's heels, ears lifted, head tilted from side to side, eager for every nuance of his voice, watching so as to follow his every movement.

'Come on, Wally.' Joe's tone makes his workroom sound exciting. Sir Walter's head is up, his tail wags as if Joe were creating his world today, especially and all for him.

Frances smiles at their companionship which obviously pleases both of them more than they know.

Better to simply enjoy than be apart enough to observe the enjoyment. She envies them a little.

She knows he's suppressing an irritability at her submersion in places he cannot fathom and something in her cries out to be released. Why can't he help her?

He doesn't even stop to ask himself why she can't be more practical. He is already beginning an arrangement before he reaches his workroom door. As he closes it, Frances and everything outside it ceases to exist, except for Wally, who settles on the rug with a sigh which breathes contentment through the room as variations on tunes begin to dance.

Frances stirs, grabs Freddie, lets him put his paws around her neck, kisses his head, listens to the rhythm of his purr, lets it vibrate through her, then carefully replacing him on the table, takes a titbit of his favourite soya cheese from the fridge and seeing him safely gratified, leaves with a purpose for her other world upstairs.

Frances picks up a green folder of notes sitting on the side of her desk. Here are snippets of history which she has extracted and collected to help her with Franziska.

Shirer wrote in 1934, *'In the background . . . there lurked the terror of the Gestapo and the fear of the concentration camp for those who got out of line or who had been communists or socialists or too liberal or too pacifist . . . Nazi terror in the early years affected the lives of relatively few – the people of this country did not seem to feel that they were being cowed by a brutal dictatorship . . . but supported it with genuine enthusiasm . . . a few former socialists or liberals or devout Christians from the old conservative classes were disgusted by the persecution of the Jews, but didn't know what to do.'*

Gestapo: Secret police. Institutional terror. *'Hitler and Goering could take the law into their own hands and the Gestapo was also the law.'*

'The first concentration camps sprang up like mushrooms during Hitler's first year of power. By the end of 1933, there were 50 of them . . . mainly to give people a good beating, then send them for ransom back to their relatives or friends. They existed mainly to terrorize people . . .'

Frances closes the file.

Franziska is waiting in Berlin. Her father has not returned. He is a liberal, a pacifist and has socialist leanings, standing resolutely against the tide of enthusiasm for the new chancellor who is holding them spellbound, but surely not a moth to their fire?

November 22nd, 1934
The world is icy cold today. Birgit has brought me hot coffee, but I can see my breath in the air as clearly as the steam from the cup. My

teeth are chattering! Birgit says I have become thinner and will fade to nothing if I don't eat up her potato pancakes. I always found them delicious, but now they have no attraction. I eat a little so as not to disappoint poor Birgit who will surely enjoy a good portion herself with their subtle onion flavour, slightly salted. She is probably licking her stout greasy fingers right now and wiping them on her apron.

November 22nd, 1934. 4.30pm
I told Birgit I was going shopping for a new dress, which considering my destination was perfectly logical. I was going to meet Fritz to collect another message. I have no way to tell him I won't be there. But here I am, my leg up in front of the fire unable to walk and sick that I might have let someone down and worry that it was something vitally important. I am sick with myself for doing this. Birgit has brought afternoon coffee and a piece of cake – which I will have to feed to the birds as I have no stomach for it now.

My mind has been turning in circles. Have I missed something very important? Who, or what plan might be endangered because I did not get to the rendezvous? Will they suspect my arrest? Not knowing who sent for me, it is impossible to get a message to them. For the first time, I have let someone down and I am helpless to rectify it.

For some silly reason my watch was slow. When I discovered this I ran along the road, slipped on a patch of ice and turned my ankle. The pain was terrible, but I didn't scream – this was surprising, considering how oversensitive I am to the least little pin-prick.

A very kind lady who reminded me of my mother brought me back home. Walking is impossible. Birgit has bathed it in salts and mustard and is muttering to herself a good deal. She brings ice, then a hot towel, saying I should be resting. I tell her I am writing to Mama, and that is very important, is it not? She nodded her head and smiled at this. I think she misses dear Mama a lot.

November 23rd, 1934

Thank God who does not desert us! Papa is home, safe and well. He came during the evening. We were so thrilled to see each other that we ate all Birgit's lovingly cooked supper into the bargain. That brought an unusually broad smile to her face.

I am at a friend's house on a bed downstairs for the present as this ankle hampers my movements. I am using an old crutch of Papa's which he used to hobble around with while getting over his injury after the war. He won't tell me where he has been – except to 'the border', but he insisted I tell him where I have been. I know he is worried now – his face looked suddenly older as he realized he was seeing as if in a mirror, a good deal of himself and smiled faintly before he shook his head and looked away.

'There are paid informers everywhere you know, Franzi,' he said. 'Along with those who do it because they relish it. Trust no-one. Write down no names. Don't use the telephone.'

'I know, I know all that,' I sighed.

'It can't be said enough. Take today. Some silly inexperienced little fool used the phone. A meeting with a courier – he was arrested along with his contact – the Gestapo were there first."

'Where, Papi?' I asked.

'Why? What does it matter? In a very public place – a smart café where no-one would suspect. They say he was new, keen, told the others there'd be another going with him, but the other one didn't turn up, it seems. It was that one's lucky day.'

I gulped. Papi saw me go white. This young man, if he was inexperienced and they questioned him, he'd give names.

He put his hand on mine. 'What is it, Franzi? What do you know?'

'Café Kristal, Kurfurstendam?' I managed to whisper.

'Dear God, we've got to get you out of here. Any friend you can go to? We'll say there's no-one to look after you with the leg.'

We moved fast. I told Papi the details in the car. 'Was the envelope sealed when you received it?'

'Of course.'

'What did you do with the note?'

'I burnt it, of course!'

'Good girl! Thank God you hurt your ankle,' was all he could say. He was calm, but I could feel his tension in my every muscle. My head was light, lifting me above panic, then he said, 'Many hours have already passed. Maybe that is a good sign, but we can't afford not to take the utmost care.' He said he won't risk going home until he finds out what has happened with the boy and if he told anyone else who was to be at the rendezvous. This poor crazy boy has put us all in danger and most of all himself.

I am staying with a sympathetic schoolfriend. The family are against the National Socialist Party and scornful of Herr Hitler, but do not talk of it. But I tell my friend nothing. Everyone thinks Mama has gone to England on a theatre engagement and I am to begin my studies at a small college of languages, where I will also learn stenography. I know only too well that what I have been involved in could mean death if any of us were found out.

My friend believes my seriousness is all to do with the pain in my ankle and is doing her best to divert me in various entertaining ways. How different this is – like another world! She chatters of clothes, romance, the kind of young man who she would like to put his arm around her on a ballroom floor, the dresses she will wear and where she will find them, what is the height of elegance in the latest fashions. She is a very attractive girl and I cannot help smiling as I imagine her in all these beautiful things, holding hands with her beau on a moonlit terrace, full of hope for a future filled with dreams.

I bring Bertie, Mama, Papa and Aunty Isabelle before me as I close my eyes, imagine them bathed in golden light, and ask the angels to protect them until these times are finished. Then I ask for the ones who have been taken, but it is hard to fight off the cold shiver down my spine. If this ankle lets me sleep, I will join my dear ones in the place of dreams.

November 26th, 1934

No message from my father yet. Even these investigations put him at risk. There will be brief, snatched meetings with people he should not be seen with in order to gain crumbs of information. I see him now, a handsome fearless hare leaping from place to place in the territory of wolves. It is a terrible irony that my joining the work might have indirectly put him in danger. But I cannot allow such thoughts to enter my head.

My friend asks so many questions – does my father have to go away on business a very great deal? It must be simply awful for me with my mother working abroad as well and no brothers and sisters. She is very kind and is genuinely concerned, yet I am glad of the release now she has gone shopping with her mother for the afternoon. Papa has a small import-export business with a friend which I'm sure helps cover what he is doing, but when Gabrielle asks all kinds of questions about what he handles, I'm unable to answer – I think she hopes he might have clothes from Paris and is not really interested in anything else. For the moment, she seems to have made him into a rather shadowy mysterious figure, an image I am trying to dispel, because that is just what he is for me also. Gabi's father is a lawyer – so very straightforward, but her parents are far too polite to ask any questions.

The doctor came. He too, was very straightforward – the ligament is slightly damaged but it's nothing that bandage, compresses and immobility won't cure. The latter makes me impatient, yet there are reasons for all things.

November 26th, 1934. 1am

I have been unable to sleep. The night is so clear and the moon so bright. Gabi came back full of stories from her expedition. Even her purchases took second place. Apparently, a small group of people had been trying to cover or erase some anti-Jewish slogans in the street when some brownshirts got hold of them. Instead of running, they foolishly fought back.

'There was blood all over their faces.' She began to cry. 'They took them away – what will happen?' I shrugged, as if I didn't know too much about such things.

'Perhaps more beating.'

'They were so brave. I cannot imagine ever being able to do such a thing, can you Franziska?'

'No,' I shook my head, but looked down for I was almost in tears because of all that was happening. 'Oh dear, is your leg hurting? Poor girl. I'll get you some hot coffee with cream.' Kind as always, Gabi rushed off to do that little service and I breathed deeply and swallowed all my feelings, and she insisted I inspect every last thing she had bought when she returned to my room.

December 1st, 1934

The first day of the last month of this eventful year, but auspicious. I am back in my own home. Papa arrived to drive me here this morning.

I couldn't wait to hear all he had to say, but we had to spend a lot of time being courteous and bidding our grateful goodbyes to Gabi and her family.

The news is good and very bad. Life so often seems to be this way – we are learning to live with the most terrible sacrifices.

My dear father did his work well. It seems the boy who had been arrested had had a heart defect from birth, but his mother had never made his personal sword of Damocles known to him. He died on the way to the police station before he could be questioned. His contact knew nothing of the third person, but is now still being held. Her relatives have been contacted – if they hand over a large sum of money, they will get him back.

And how did he have my name?

He'd got hold of a list. Some fool had written down names – five in all but not the addresses. A woman of my name has been arrested – she comes from another district, the other side of Berlin – part of an anti-fascist catholic group.

This lad was something of a rebel, it seems, with a will of his own. His father is a school inspector who is friendly with Fräulein Niemeier – my name had perhaps been mentioned after the incident with her. He obviously made assumptions about my reputation, gained from the schoolmistress – overheard at dinner, perhaps, and imagined I was the catholic anti-fascist. This does not put me out of danger, for it means a name which fits me is now on the Gestapo's list.

This wild young maverick had confided in an associate of Fritz, who had naturally denied any knowledge of anything and had seen to it that the list of names was destroyed, but a copy had already gone astray. He had big ideas about planning the escape of one of that group and had taken things dangerously into his own hands. To us, it sounded more like foolhardy rebellion against the father. Now, still a teenager, he has paid with his life.

I am to go to Aunt Isabelle's in the country, to keep away, at least until I can walk properly again. Papa is to drive me tomorrow. We are both still feeling numb from the knowledge of my narrow escape.

A friend of my father's is leaving for England. We are writing to Mama, telling her I am fine and continuing my studies. We mention nothing of our dramas and send presents to remind her of us. I hope she will find plenty of her own kind of drama to keep her occupied, cheerful and fulfilled so far away from us. If she cannot work as an actress, she will be fretful and all the powerful energy will waste and eat at her soul. Surely that will not happen...

April 14th, 1935

Although I have often felt guilty and disappointed, being out here in the country, unable to get around and having simply to rest, I have had no option but to study. My foreign language textbooks are well-thumbed and my aunt leaves me alone for hours each day to do the things I wish to do. I have written some poems for Bertie, but cannot send him a single line. This is very difficult, but the joy came in writing them.

It seems that when I fell, I managed to unbalance my spine and the leg and ankle are now taking a long while to heal. Rest has been the prescription, but I have also devised some of my own exercises from watching how the dogs and cats stretch themselves and always move with such freedom and grace. Oh to be as free in the body as they are!

We must be thankful for small mercies. This injury has kept me away from the pressures of the state. Everywhere young people are being pressed into the Hitler Youth. It is horrible to see groups of empty-headed girls singing away on the farms here, gladly taking their fill of all the toxic propaganda pumped into them. Our nation is in a fever, its life-blood swarms with germs so virulent and sickening, that death surely threatens. Our culture is rapidly becoming desiccated and will crumble to dust before this mighty and merciless machine.

Aunty and I take care and stand back and analyse carefully all that we read in the newspapers, all that we hear on the wireless. Papa has tutored us well. We shall not be tainted by the miasma which creeps like a yellow sulphurous fog under the doors and through the cracks in the window frames of every household in this land.

I see now, listening to Papa and Bertie, the Nazis have pushed into every corner of our lives. We are no longer free. We are required to make a pact with the devil and so many are tempted, but the devil, in the end, will need to destroy them. We, too, must wear masks, for many have breathed deeply of this fog, taken it into their lungs, and now its sticky fumes course through their veins. Hoodwinked by their own grey vulnerability, their eyes gleam darkly. We must deliver supreme performances in this dangerous play. Now it is more than the Fischers we must be wary of. Any unchecked trust would simply be stupidity. People everywhere are encouraged to spy, to denounce, to presume sinister deeds of one another. The Nazis are slicing through families, cutting lovers' knots and breaking the bonds of friendship. In tyranny, none shall be safe. We are dealing with lives.

A message has come from my dear father. He is to arrive tomorrow with a surprise, but his code says be careful, let no one see anything: 'A special treat that I am certain you won't want to share.' I have to think of what it might be, but stop myself and try to concentrate on my studies and bang away on the typewriter to drown all speculative thoughts.

April 18th, 1935

I was not disappointed! Papa brought Bertie here. He was with us all day yesterday. I was not at all surprised but simply thrilled and relieved after so long. Not a single message in all this time and suddenly, there he was! We hurried them into the house, but our excited questions met only with silent smiles and shaking of the head. 'Where have you been?' 'Where did you manage to meet?' 'Have you come from Berlin today?' I should have known better, but the excitement blew all thoughts of caution from my mind. We are still safe!

I fear more and more, sitting here, though I shut the thought away into a twilight corner of my mind, that Bertie is a marked man and now, all too easily recognized. Sometimes I hear the warning, 'Only a matter of time,' as if the devils are at our heels and I chase them away with plans for the future, a future where beautiful truth will rise again and the lies will lie forsaken and forgotten in the dust.

I took Bertie to my room and showed him my studies and how well I can type. In these strange times this could be considered dangerous, to possess a typewriter, but I must study alone at home. Bertie is so unhappy at all the discomfort the injury caused, but has it not had its compensations? I tell him it is far worse that I have been so unable to help him. At this, he produced some documents for me to translate, papers which not even Aunty must know about. Besides, what she doesn't know can't harm her. I am to give the documents hidden in a box containing a gift, to someone who will be at the local station in three days' time. I read the anxiety in his face as he handed me the papers, but hoped that my delight would break that small cloud and send it well away. I know the rules. So far, I have never made a mistake.

Papa and Aunty left us alone for a very long time, understanding how much we need to talk, to be with each other. I so wanted, but did not ask, why he had sent no message in so long. However, eventually, dear Bertie told me how things had been very difficult in recent months and what is more, after my narrow escape, he felt it best there should be no possible thread leading back to me. No one has managed to discover the eventual tale of the woman of my name who was taken. They have tried, but failed. It was as if a curtain had been drawn. She has disappeared into the labyrinths. Perhaps she is already dead. 'In some cases,' Bertie said, 'we have no choice but to walk on.' I shivered as a cold finger ran down my spine. Who is this, my echo, walking as in the dimmed and endless corridors of this dusky spectred time which makes strangers of friends and saviours of strangers? Superimposed upon each other by our names, for moments, fate pointed its finger at our composite form, but fate's finger split us apart and gave us different new days to wake in.

When I pressed Bertie to tell me about something of their prisons

– as if I could not imagine – he refused. What guilt was I trying to assuage for the one who had been taken in my place?

'It is cruel, but thank God they didn't get you,' Bertie said as he took my face in his hands and gave me a kiss which dissolved the earth and took us weightless, swirling through space, and into the ethereal light of the Milky Way. I wished that he would never leave and for a few moments wondered how much longer we would survive, living under such torment, torn apart, relying upon faith and our beliefs to sustain us. It was as if our lives were as fragile as rice paper and might break at the touch of a hand and yet, and yet, we both have rods of unbending steel at our very core which cannot be broken.

I know that according to the rules of this uncertain time, I should not be committing these things to paper. We know their ways. Should suspicion ever fall, Aunty's house or our home would be stripped and every possible hiding place laid bare. And yet, my inner voice has told me, my dreams have told me, that I must. Because of this, I believe my pages will be protected by the Light.

I looked up at Bertie as we sat quietly in the room and saw the light around him, just for a moment or two. This was a sign to me. We are something extraordinary to one another and not even the hand of death itself could part us.

At first, he seemed to smile less than usual and I feared that something may have caused his feelings to change during these empty months. But as we talked, he warmed and it was the tension of so much care which fell away from him like so many heavy weights and allowed his face to lighten once again. I saw that mysterious shine in his brilliant and beautiful blue eye. I listened intently to the steady low note of his voice. Most of all I savoured the silences between us.

Finally, I gathered enough confidence in his return to offer him one of the better poems. I held my breath, waiting, every muscle held tightly unmoving as he read it through two, perhaps three times. Waiting.

Then he looked up. He told me he would carry it in his breast pocket forever as he put his arms around me, kissing the top of my head. And stillness came upon us and an unseen power flared through our veins and there was new life in us.

He would not give me the smallest crumb of information about where he has been. I know he is right to be silent, for all our sakes, and yet it is hard simply to have to imagine and to wonder day after uncertain day.

Now that I have seen him again, looked closely, felt and heard his voice, he will be nearer when he is away. Time always clouds memory however hard we try to polish and preserve it as though it were a diamond beyond price. Like all things of this world, it cannot, will not, hold its place into an infinite future. The fading of a face holds the sorrow of all losses and yet, in some higher realm than ours, there is no loss.

At lunch, we joked and laughed as if we were all in a magic bubble, isolated from the world around us, and then we drank to Mama and the bubble burst for a moment and allowed thoughts and talk of heavier things to enter. But by the time we sipped coffee from Aunty's delicate Dresden cups, we were full of renewed hope that the beast might yet be driven back and defeated if only we could awaken enough minds to its threat and if only those in other countries would realize and support us.

Later, in the full of the afternoon, Bertie and I went into the garden and I showed him the first seeds sown in the rich, dark earth and there we made a secret vow to one another. There will never be anyone else for us and summer will come and the earth will offer up her endless gifts and swallows will fly and swoop, writing our promise in the sky.

'*Liebe ist fur uns nur einmal.*' Love for us comes but once. We spoke the words, first separately, and then together, looking into each other's eyes. Then an infinite stillness. Silence. A pair of ringed doves flew past, one calling to the other, the first silent, the second calling, calling.

April 24th, 1935
Today I shall deliver more documents to the station. I feel impatient to be back in Berlin, playing a greater part in the work. The impatience grew as I sifted through my own private papers. Amongst them I came across a small cutting from last year – a strange coincidence that I should turn it up on this very day: an extract from the new Law of April 24th last year:

> '... Whoever attempts to maintain in existence means of organizations (continuing the maintenance of a party) ... whoever attempts to influence the masses by the publication and distribution of written matter
> ... WILL BE PUNISHED WITH DEATH.'

I am hiding my papers in a new place today, a place which not even the cleverest mind would think of. It was shown to me in a dream last night. And the dream woke me in the early hours of the morning. And I was not afraid.

June 21st, 1935. Midsummer Day
I walked out into the moonlight last night, unusually unable to sleep and there was a coldness in its glow as if our fate is sealed. I felt the sorrow of the almost lifeless moon and knew that she had given of herself long, long ago. Stepping into her silver embrace, I felt I was part of a sacrifice upon an ancient alter, ancient beyond counting. A bird cried out in the soundless silver glow and I shivered as if it had called my name across the night sky, a messenger to the stars, the moonlight a shroud, an army of demons waiting for the satanic command. I stood between two worlds and the life of my soul depended upon

the strength it could summon at this terrible hour – the demons were waiting to swallow it whole. I prayed for power to withstand. I knew I should not sleep until sunrise, that I must fight for my immortal soul. I summoned Bertie's smile as if we were each the guardian angel of the other. I chanted childhood prayers and prayers which presented themselves to my mind riven in two halves, one calm and strong, the other in utter torment unto madness and awaited the release of the dawn.

When it came, I slept, exhausted, until half of the new day was spent. I wondered at this trial that echoes from a past which reverberates across an infinite sea of dreams and I wonder what spectres rise like ghostly armies at the trumpet call of destiny, shadows aeons old.

The monster tramples our freedoms like flowers crushed beneath heavy boots, yet see how the tiniest flowers push their growth from behind the heaviest stones to meet the life-giving sun and rain. If they are torn away, they come again, born anew. Their vital strength in all that minute fragility is greater than the thickest, heaviest, human hand which can never curse the truth of their beauty.

August 30th, 1935
This will be brief today. My hand trembles as I write. I will be leaving tomorrow and must pack my belongings. Aunty is resting, nursing her bruises. I must go to her again in a few moments. I left her in a fitful sleep, murmuring Papa's name.

The SA brownshirt thugs woke us at four this morning, banging on the doors. When Aunty opened up, they burst in, three men, one like a weasel with spectacles, one tall, stocky and overbearing, the other a blur, knocking her over, pushing and banging and one of them shouting through his teeth. Then they began to turn the place upside down. Every drawer, every cupboard, every box was turned out. This house is so beautifully polished and orderly and apart from Aunty's neatly arranged books, there are no papers stacked away. After two hours they found nothing and two of them, overcome by frustration, grabbed us and spat their poisoned threats in our faces. I was thrown across a chair. Aunty, afraid for my back, screamed and ran to help me, but was given more bruises for her trouble. She is convinced one of the villagers has fabricated some malicious story about me for it was obvious they were not particularly interested in her, but for the fact that I was in her house.

Perhaps one of those who are avidly joining the drive for 'Jew-free villages' and somehow suspect my looks – for I have not re-dyed my hair in all these months – attempted to denounce us.

Aunt Isabelle is an honoured, respected and well-liked member of this small community. I cannot believe she could have a single enemy in the world. For both our sakes, I can no longer stay here.

A dear friend is helping the maid clear the chaos the men left behind them. She is clucking in concern, anxiety and disbelief.

This makes my heart the heavier and seals my lips yet tighter but the tightness which covers my heart is involuntary and pains me beyond telling.

I am packing my things, placing all my belongings in the suitcase, every movement automatic. My head is clear and yet I walk in clouds of cotton wool as if the floorboards did not make one creak beneath my stepping feet.

This trail of chaos is their message, mark and threat. I must fly. This nest can no longer be home. The broken wing is mended. Bertie, I am calling our promise across the sky. Hear me, for thoughts are words with wings.

Aunty advises I leave because she feels it will be safer for me. I insist I go because I feel it will be safer for her. I have become 'a wanderer in a strange land'.

It must have been an angel who told me where to hide my papers not in the house. So we were saved.

As this summer slips into autumn, I know I shall be well enough to resume the work. Let not the frost bite us when winter comes.

September 1st, 1935
There were tears in our eyes as we parted at the station today. Aunty was wearing a grey costume which mirrored the grey shadows beneath her green eyes. She walked slowly, the bruises impeding her movements and I felt a weight of guilt for every painful step. Our concerns were for each other as we embraced. Love renders our enemy powerless. We close him without in our togetherness. Even the clouds were grey today as we breathed *'Aufwiedersehen'* the air so still, the late summer sun in hiding.

September 2nd, 1935
I believe I may have become a master of the impassive expression. Aloof, young, alone, I read studiously on the train – my textbooks for translation. Beneath my dress thumped a heart which felt as if its unremarkable owner were carrying a mine buried in the secret compartments of her bag that touched, might explode. Somehow, I feel this little message will gain a life of its own and tenacious of that life, will not allow its destruction or neglect.

March, 1936
Much has been done in these last months, but our work has become even more difficult. Bertie and I have managed to meet from time to time but the meetings are always so brief. His manner has changed. Confident in the world – he has so far escaped so much – he has lost his former spontaneity, out of necessity, I know. But I watch him melt once more as we spend time together, our nearness a balm to the chafing of the armour we must wear against this alien world.

He moves constantly, and, I believe, travels a good deal. Never stay in one place for long is a fundamental rule for an activist in our movement. And watch. Watch behind you, in front of you, to the right and to the left. Papa and I may soon be forced to become nomadic too. Already we have moved – to an apartment in a different part of town.

It was sad to leave our home with all of its memories now locked within its closed doors. My throat aches with emotion when I think of the love of family and friends which breathed in its walls, the animated chatter of dinner parties which hummed in the rooms. Yet bricks and mortar are not to be clung to. These are days of expediency and extremes.

Birgit is staying with us for the time being. She is getting older, and soon she may have to go to live with family in the country. Meanwhile we are sure her loyalty is to be trusted but we speak nothing of the work. She worships Papa like a faithful dog.

I am ashamed to say I cried when we finally closed the door and looked back along the pathway for the last time – I knew there would be no return – but I was thinking of Mama and how those who long to be together are parted. I looked down at the dark flecked hue of my woollen dress and said to myself, this sombre attire is fitting; this is not a day for rejoicing. We are saying goodbye to a life which will not be again. I allowed these thoughts to intrude upon a sweeter voice which insisted uselessly, 'But change must come, do not resist the inevitable. The rose does not cling vainly to summer; it fades with dignity to the rhythm of the shortening days. But the Divine love which created it fades not for a single moment.'

Father's face was set without a smile as he gave calm orders to the men who carried away our belongings. They obeyed his every word with the utmost respect on their faces, these simple men, while Birgit fussed behind, always mindful of Papa's wellbeing. This is the effect he has upon people.

He has an unspoken authority which is born of a wellspring of love for his fellow man. Anger is alien to him, except when faced with the beast, and then it speaks in silence.

My last walk from the door to the road was slow, in the manner of reflection. I stopped for a moment and looked up into the flowering cherry tree bursting with spring-time ebullience and caught a glimpse of heaven in the voluptuousness of its pink blossoms. I let it gather me up and sighed. Then suddenly, stepping back into time, I looked around and caught Birgit's watery eyes upon me, grey-ringed in the ageing pink-grey-whiteness of her face. She looked away as I snapped one sweet crisp narcissus from the patch Mama had planted with such joy three years before.

Drinking its scent, I threaded its hollow stalk, leaking sticky juice through my buttonhole and turned with purpose towards the gate. Where shall we go? I sat in silence beside Papa as he drove our black car. Shall we become like rabbits burrowing underground, chased, hounded? Many already have been bagged – vermin, bleeding, screaming, captive or dead. Sing blackbird, sing your sweetest requiem. They are dying. They are dying. Carry the message skylark, carry it to the heavens. Who shall listen now?

Since last month the Gestapo have absolute powers – they are making arrests with no necessity of referring to the courts. They are now a law unto themselves – for the good of the Fatherland! We have taken another large step towards the abyss of tyranny.

Yet still we hope, and work, and resist and hope and drink deeply of Hope's eternal spring.

There are moments when I long to rest from this tension, my nerves poised upon the brink of breaking. And thus I sleep and in the realms beyond our dreams, these fragile nerves find recovery and hope once more the next day will be new.

But tomorrow, who knows what dangers tomorrow threatens in a world of tyranny?

Chapter 14

Anxiety over the rescued dogs is close to overwhelming Frances. She feels compelled to call Pamela to ask if there is any news, but is unsure if Pam's telephone is safe. A courageous rescuer, she has never been caught because she is clever, intelligent, and very aware and brave. They cannot afford to take any risks. Suspecting a tap recently, Pamela had set up a phoney rescue meeting on the telephone and had turned up at the place at the time arranged, checked as if innocent, to find police waiting. Case proven. Frances will ask her to call back. She will know what that means.

It is Sunday afternoon. Joe wants a family outing. She asks him to be patient for a few minutes. She goes to call in his studio. The number rings and rings as Joe paces, impatient. Finally, an answer.

'Pam? It's me – can you call back ASAP?'

'Okay. Five minutes.'

She knows what Frances means.

Animal liberationists are considered 'terrorists', especially of late. No one has ever been killed but the movement has its own martyrs. Who are those creating the terror? Their activities are condoned by law, just as the Brownshirts were allowed to pillage and plunder peoples' homes, because the victims were helpless. Animals cannot defend themselves against the cunning minds of humans who justify any terrible act to suit their selfish desires. Frances waits, on edge. Joe is still pacing. The call comes soon enough, however.

'Any news?'

'I haven't heard anything, but I'm worried. I saw that copper off pretty quickly when he came here. Considering I do so much of their work for them locally with cruelty cases, I should think so. He was a young one and none too bright.'

Pam's sharp mind and wit could run rings around a plod. But still, Frances is uneasy. 'I can't help but be anxious.'

'I'll make some enquiries.'

'Thanks, I have a strange feeling -'

'Okay. I'll call you if and when.' She hangs up.

Joe elects for an afternoon out by the river. 'No nervous breakdowns,' he warns as he steers everyone plus dogs into the Renault estate, dogs in the back, excited and whining with anticipation.

The air is cold today. Frances turns the car heater up but a cold electric shiver runs down her spine. She quickly dismisses it and puts on a mood of cheer. Joe is telling a silly joke and looks to see her reaction. She obliges with a broad smile, despite what is going on inside her. She will not pull everyone down into the abyss of her vague, amorphous fears. The world needs joy and here and now she has some very real love around her, like a comforting blanket.

They go along the river and have tea in a place which serves toast with home-made jam, reminding her of her young days when tea rooms were a feature of most English towns and villages. It is somehow comforting that some good things can last.

When they get back, someone is parked on the drive. He steps out as they drive in. Frances is surprised. 'Phil! What are you doing here?'

'Asking you a favour, just for a night or two.'

'Come in.'

They sit in the kitchen and make tea. The boys have gone upstairs.

'I've jumped bail,' Phil says. 'I was going to ask to stay for a night or two, hide out, while I sort my mind.'

Phil is well known in Animal Liberation, but he's done nothing really criminal. The Conspiracy Law is being used to net them in.

Joe says nothing, but silently sets about making dinner. Frances can feel his objection so chats to block it out.

'You can stay here, fugitive from our wonderful justice,' she laughs.

Joe can't hold back. 'The police were here – they could well be back. They were checking round the house –'

'The dogs you got out,' Phil knows, doesn't have to be told.

'Yes,' Frances says, 'I'm worried for their safety.'

'Don't blame you,' Phil says. 'Not everyone can be trusted.'

When dinner is ready, they call the boys and eat in the kitchen. Phil entertains them well. They talk about adventurous things. Phil runs marathons and climbs mountains. The dogs sit round the table and are given their supply of tidbits. Lord Cecil Llewellyn puts his head on the table and burps in appreciation. Everyone thinks it hilarious.

When Phil has gone to his bedroom, Joe tackles Frances.

'This is a very real risk, you know – harbouring someone on bail.'

'It's the least we can do. Anyway, he's not a criminal,' Frances insists.

'No, he just assists those who break the law.'

'The bad laws. Those who free the prisoners. You know the deal. Is it right?'

'No.'

'Then we help the resistors.' Joe is silent.

'You know, I sat on the press bench at a conspiracy trial recently. The evidence was appallingly thin. Then a man was called into the witness box – he was perhaps in his forties. He was asked if it were right to damage property. He said, "If I broke into a concentration camp and smashed their instruments of torture, I believe I would be on the side of 'right and good'." I could never ever forget it.'

Joe was silent. 'I know, but if that policeman turns up again tomorrow to get his precious CD signed, we're right in it –'

'Let's see what tomorrow brings,' Frances says. 'The spirit of Torquemada is not yet laid to rest and I would gladly help throw it into the abyss.'

Joe turns away and puts the light out.

Shadows play on the walls. Shades cast themselves across Frances's mind. Next morning, Joe is tense and Phil feels it.

'I've thought about you being under suspicion,' he says. 'I'll move on, but thanks very much for last night and not sending me off.'

Frances tells him he doesn't have to go. There is a tense moment, but his mind is made up.

Joe is too effusive when Phil departs.

Two weeks later, Frances gets news that Phil turned himself in. Prison is mightily unpleasant but Phil made the best of it and was going to use it to study. She felt very proud of him.

'Not all prisoners are criminals,' Frances says to Joe after breakfast, 'and not all laws are good. So long as there are innocent prisoners, none of us are free.'

Joe just smiles and takes a sip of coffee.

Chapter 15

Frances is lying in bed, in white linen pyjamas enjoying the smooth, cool, crisp whiteness of Egyptian cotton sheets, grateful for the comfort of a firm pillow beneath her head. A weariness has taken hold of her. She doesn't move. Freddie is a large, soft ball under the duvet beside her. He has fallen into a deep, comfortable, inert sleep. She runs the long thin fingers of her right hand across the contours of his supple spine and wishes for thoughts which would flow and bend as easily with the changing currents of life.

The China tea Joe brought her fifty minutes ago has quickly aged into a bitter coldness. It stands, untouched upon the bedside table. She hates this inertia which grips her, which points a knowing finger at life slipping past her, but she needs the stillness.

Not even the shouts, laughter, music and high spirits sparking up the stairs from the family below can tempt her into movement or draw her into a desire to join them. Joe has a friend staying – an old friend, a solid, devoted one, whose attention now replaces her. She is enjoying the respite from the responsibility of being a good companion. Frances needs to be remote today, in a world apart from everyday demands.

They are crunching the warm crusts of Joe's freshly baked bread, dripping with melting margarine, piled with fruit-filled jam, locked into eager, laughing conversation, interrupted only by mouthfuls of hot French coffee. Joe's brown eyes, smiling, cannot call her. She wants to be alone.

She reaches back to the night of the rescue and replays each scene. She soon finds Black Dog, the chief player, and looks into his dark eyes, catches their soft yearning. A slight smile lights her face.

What mystery took hold and led me by the hand to effect our fatal introduction, Dear Dog? She asks, purposely slowing her thoughts, the better to contemplate the extraordinary complexity which is the spirit of a dog who arrived one dark night, a stranger in her life, and speaking to her soul, said, 'Old friends and dear to each other.'

Frances frowns at this unquestionable truth. Just as strange humans may by some invisible quality become instant, familiar, dear and trusted friends, a creature too might rise above the tide of life, reach out, and be recognized by the one who has eyes to see.

A dog barks sharply. Frances starts. Excited barks. Two dogs. Frances is jolted out of the reverie. The boys and friends, a pack with the dogs, are running in and out of the garden. The dogs are infected with enthusiasm for the game. The boys, their faces red and shiny with the energy of childhood are lost in play – the pure pleasure of it. It is an imaginary world where everything bounces back. That is the electric charge of childhood. Nothing flags nor fades, even tiredness is a mere intake of breath before the next race.

Joe and his friend don't hear the commotion. They are sealed off in a world of memories which amuse, events rehashed, re-tinted, re-shot in slapstick to entertain. Shared laughter bounces off the kitchen walls and feeds the atmosphere of excitement in which the dogs are leaping, a sparkling tune to which they dance, lost in the moment.

Three worlds exist in this house in this frothy-clouded morning pierced by an insistent sun. Three worlds, their inhabitants all in a communion of their own, three worlds separate and apart, yet laid across each other, each transparent, so interwoven are they, each unable to fully exist without the other, translucent in their energy and each ignorant of a myriad other worlds which touch and overlay their own.

Frances yearns for the energy of those new to life, a wistful yearning free of envy, born of a delighted admiration for its freshness – for freshness reaches nearer the state of perfection and innocence. The children and the dogs – their oneness with the living moment. She longs to feel that much alive, but instead counts, counts the lines of lead which trace the pattern of stained glass on the window – a measure of her anxiety. The counting pushes back the incoming tide, blots it into nothingness. Just childish counting, one, two, three, four. Repeat. Count again. Resist. The sun breaks through and makes the colours shine.

She swallows the ruby red and midnight blue into her soul and regains peace. A moment of regeneration.

'Are you coming with us?' Joe's voice is alive with bonhomie. Frances has drifted on the sea of her dreams. Wally, looking first at Joe, his object of devotion, pursues his question, puts his muddy front paws upon the pristine sheet, is panting eagerly in her face.

Wally is laughing, two lines of white teeth, pink tongue dangling. Frances cannot find it in her to tell him off, only a mild resigned amusement. There are times when disengagement becomes obligatory. Life is happening to Frances. Having waded too far out, she is now floating, feeling the sun, the clouds, rain, as if nothing were a part of her.

'We're taking the boys – and the dogs –' Joe's voice comes as if from a distance. He stands tall above her, smiling.

Frances puts a hand to her head. A sharp pain stabs knife-like into its left side.

'You didn't drink your tea! Some more?' Joe is bending over her. Frances shakes her head. Confusion holds her tightly in its tentacled arms. 'We'll come back and collect you for a late lunch – how about that?' Frances nods, smiles and repeats the required answer already supplied, 'Yes, a little later.'

Joe is invigorated. His friend is his world now. He forgets to kiss his wife goodbye. She watches his movements. He's relaxed, flexing like an athlete enjoying his body. He's not with her. A twinge of guilt flickers in her mind. Her husband is thrilled at the attention, the equal division of sharing the moment with his friend, like a child who has managed to secure the full and absolute attention of a parent. She's neglected him through these weeks and months of her own private dramatic tragedy with a cast of millions. She has been submerged and he could not reach her. Each time he stretched a hand or braved the waves, they carried her away – she silent, he calling.

She looks up, wanting to reassure, but he's already a disappearing figure, half cut by the door. It closes. Silence. Her connection is cut off. She panics for a moment. Then relief comes. She'll retreat. Freddie hasn't moved. He purrs as he feels her movement as she settles to drift into a gentle sleep in order to remake the day.

Joe, shoulders straight and square, hands in the pockets of his indigo dyed linen jeans, bounces down the wide polished treads of the oak staircase, past the rampant lion at its foot and goes to gather the pack. Wally's tail, up and straight, wags his whole rear end with doggish laughter.

Frances listens to the departure – wheels scrunch the gravel. She is sad and relieved, her head submerged in Freddie's purr, reaching for a recreation of the day.

The jolt back into wakefulness is shocking. Frances is carrying the weight of a dream drawn through the windows of consciousness into the light of day. It is the shadow of the evil which Franziska bore. She has been looking into its face, feeling the horror of its freezing sinewed hands gripping at her throat, locking her into silence.

But Frances has spirit stronger than this visitation, this sinister shadow rising from its grave.

Banishment is in her hands.

She leaps up, turns to fill the house with Bach's *Toccata and Fugue* in D minor. She feels the organ-pipes filling her with their reverberating fullness, revitalizing every cell with melodies of glorious splendour. This music of the heavens chases the face of hell away.

Lunch in the country hotel is frivolous with laughter, a rejoining of worlds. Now Joe has everyone, for Frances has reset herself to meet them on their terms, to ignore the stabbing, aching, dragging pains which gnaw at her edges and smiles. She sits upright, echoes of Egypt draped in the geometric lines of her turquoise cotton dress. The two men are drawn in. She jokes and teases and Joe is full with comfortable familiarity returned.

This place is old and comfortably not too tidy. Frances loves age, left a little rough and wild at the edges. The boys run out on to the lawns; their stomachs full of strawberry banana ices. The three sit on the terrace, looking out on to all this green and weathered red brick and stone, flanked by tall trees, some stalwart green, others turned ochre and sienna with centuries of history locked in their breathing solidity. Beyond, a field of long grass is patterned with splendid patches of cream frothy lace meadowsweet and bright strands of purple loosestrife. The hedge is abundantly strewn with beautiful and delicate dog roses recalling the lines of Rupert Brooke:

> *Unkempt about those hedges blows,*
> *An unofficial English rose.*

The ancestor of her favourite flowers to which Gerard the sixteenth-century herbalist gave 'the most principal place among all flowers'. Frances could not but agree.

Red valerian sprouts in prolific joy through the grey rocks of the stone wall, its pink flowers profuse; and ice plant, its succulent leaves plump with stored water. The sky shines a watery, wispy blue. There is a satisfying delicacy in the light. The men's green and blue tweedy heavy linen jackets are restfully comfortable on Frances's searching eye. There are moments when her effort is rewarded tenfold now. There is a mutuality which seems too flexible and strong ever to be broken. It is as if the same blood runs through their veins; they are nourished by the same air, fed from the same heart. Frances, Joe and Simon, Joe's mentor, confidant hero and friend.

To break the veins of friends, Frances is thinking. This trust is long lost to those who pillage love.

The dogs are playing with the boys on the lawns. The knees of new-pressed jeans stain green as they wrestle; excited barks, calls and shouts mingle. Black Dog waits. Does he hope? Does a dog know a future or is a dog always locked in the room of now? Black Dog waits, hidden in the twilight between the world of captivity and the world of freedom.

Did Franziska, Bertie and Pauli know these moments in their twilight world, sustained by hope? Frances sees the three living ghosts superimposed upon the we three now and invites them to share this green freedom, to breathe the air of a borrowed world. She borrows theirs and they borrow hers and both belong.

She invites Black Dog to join the game, puts him on the grass to join 'chase the ball'. He leaps and flies and pants and twists in the air, lithe and free. And he belongs. Frances embraces this company of friends and the coffee is warm in her chest as she swallows; the room and the gardens are filled with a strange light which she cannot and does not describe. She is in it and it is in her, they are the light. Simon and Joe smile the smile of two who know but do not understand. But for now, knowing is enough because the place is deep and strong and the mind will not tarnish its pristine glow.

Later that evening as the three sit together in each other's glow, the house still of the noise and banter and clatter of children and dogs, still with their quiet breathing in cherubic sleep. Alone, they allow themselves to talk of what troubles them. Like conspirators, they confide over the rescue of the dogs. They chew over the remains of Frances's painful bitterness, of the anger which heats her blood and lights her eyes with fire. She tells the story of the ravaged and the saved, to save herself from an insanity which threatens should the tide of anguish engulf her. She remembers the beagle bitches who came to live with them, sad dogs with huge, sad eyes, enforced progenitors of an endless stream of dead victims in this ceaseless war of worlds where none can be healed. All their puppies had gone to be experimented upon. And no babies shall be saved.

Joe's friend, a born actor, speaks the lines of MacNeice like a native, giving voice to Frances' silence:

> *I am not yet born; provide me*
> *With water to dandle me, grass to grow for me, trees to talk*
>   *to me, sky to sing to me, birds and a white light*
>   *in the back of my mind to guide me.*

The tears which glisten in her eyes swell the volume of his rich, deep voice as he calls out to the stars which speckle the glinting deep of midnight:

> *I am not yet born, O hear me,*
> *Let not the man who is beast or who thinks he is God come near me.*

In their joining of worlds, fear melts to reward the swelling heart of courage which reaches to the stars.

And the white light makes all things possible. There is no darkness which cannot be cancelled when the white light shines.

And all is gathered up and pain becomes an unremembered past instead of a future to be faced with trepidation.

Three become one and those invisible strangers who Frances draws in become one with them; there is joyful laughter in the silence which sits so comfortably upon them now.

Frances calls Franziska. Franziska answers across time and waits till morning comes, waits patiently upon the desk.

When it comes, two hands write and are joined.

November, 1938
In the second week of this month, horror came. Jews were burned, raped and murdered, in synagogues, homes and streets, even as they fled. All that we have foreseen is coming to pass. We live among monsters who have been allowed to flourish, grown out of the shadows, they confront us at every turn. An iron mesh weaves through and grips our nation and there is no escape.

Chapter 16

Simon has departed. The routine of daily life has returned. Frances feels anxiety building inexorably, sorry for Joe that the mortar which binds its chaotic nerve-tangled bricks, holding her into herself, hems her into the worlds she has chosen to inhabit with the ones who seek life through her pen.

Joe's well-intentioned suggestions intrude. 'Take a break – a walk? a ride?'

She wants to do those things. But alone. The food he cooks she leaves in pieces on her plate. He attempts to engage her with the news. She turns off the radio, avoids the television room, glances at the newspapers, but turns away.

She forces an interest in school marks, teachers' gripes and flares at an unfair detention imposed upon her spirited eldest, gives up on a mountain of odd socks and throws away the ones which have grown holes.

She clears out a room to reduce the chaos in her mind and sends Joe, smiling at last, with loaded bags, to the charity shop. He loves to unload, throw out, give away. Sometimes she fears he wants to take her thoughts and sort them – those she may keep, others for the rubbish heap, compost, like the old sandwiches in their small son's pockets.

No one shall order her mind. She fights against his will, unsure who he wants to do this for. She crumbles at the thought that all motives might be selfish. It's an idea which diminishes everything and she banishes it. She knows that it is because of those thoughts that Franziska and the Black Dog are so important to her. Because of them, she glimpses the strength which grows beyond the helplessness imposed by circumstance. It is a yearning which drives her on and makes her reach further.

Dear Dog, another sleepless night has passed. I woke in the early hours, sobbing violently. Thankfully, it was this that shook me into wakefulness and out of the nightmare.

I had been running through darkened streets – narrow and oppressive, the buildings tall and grey on either side, each empty window a gaping opacity, sinister with vague threat. I was running, stumbling, looking for you in all this emptiness so crowded with evil. I had to find you, but knew I was running for my life with an unknown enemy in pursuit.

Eventually, after turning many corners, I came upon a small public garden and there, on a patch of grass, I saw you. I called out and fell on my knees beside you. At that moment I saw that there was no life left in your body. In disbelief I cried out and lifted your head which lay heavily in my hands. It was then that I saw that the maggots were already eating into the dead flesh.

This mark of utter finality and certain decay overwhelmed me with grief. It became like a wall through which I could never pass. I began to weep uncontrollably and that is how I emerged from the dream, back into the waking world.

I got up as if the very act of moving from the bed would shake away the experience, and picking up my watch, walked out into the corridor. It was 2.30 in the morning, First, I wandered from room to room as if sleepwalking, and then went to the garden to breathe the chilled night air, hoping that it might cleanse away the clinging greyness of fear.

The moon was almost full and I shuddered involuntarily as a shadowy cloud passed across its face. An owl hooted in the stillness. I sat on a stone wall and listened to the night, waiting for nature to speak to me in her own way, but the deadness and the worms and the pursuing evil clung tenaciously to the corners of my mind. Eventually, the cold cut through to my consciousness and with one last pleading look at the huge old oak tree, shivering, I moved back into the house and back to bed. My mind numbed, I managed to retrieve a restless and fitful sleep. The world is quite different this morning. I woke to streaked sunlight and with a tingling sense of approaching early autumn in the air. I have been listening to the birds chattering noisily in the attic since dawn and now some especially lively ones are bursting their hearts with song in the trees, their branches emerging steadily from the mist. A single cloud hangs in the valley.

There is a busily contented hum of wild bees outside the bedroom window which makes me especially happy. They have a hive just inside the roof and several of them lay dying in my room one warm day last winter. They had gone out to forage too soon and unfed, were struggling home exhausted. One by one, I lifted them to the windowsill and fed them with honey until they were all revived.

It was so thrilling. They were pulled back from the hands of death which already clutched them. It had been such a delicate operation, the tips of my fingers being larger than their small bodies.

At least it would have been a natural death, without a trace of evil.

Man is made the agent of evil, the manufacturer of pain. Fighting against this heritage is hell.

My hopeful musings this morning ended upon such a gloomy note and I feel I owe it to you not to perpetrate such heavy and painful thoughts which can only serve to drag us down deeper into the slough of despond. If I am truly honest, I can say with truth in this moment of renewed strength, that I have always found redemption somehow much nearer in the darkest and most hopeless moments. I think this comes at the point of refusal to accept total darkness and refusal to turn away and flee: the pledge to stumble on over the threshold of ultimate pain – physical, mental, emotional, spiritual, whatever form the suffering takes.

That is why, this afternoon, it feels very necessary to say, yes, such a heritage is Hell. But building strength towards wholeness, we have a chance to overcome. It really is pointless to complain about it, to feel sorry for oneself. You see, I know that you did neither of those things. I saw in your eyes that neither anger nor self-pity were possible for you.

That makes me feel so unutterably humble.

At this point I must stop the train of thought, otherwise it will degenerate into self-hatred for all the human shortcomings which are an inevitable part of me. I would rather finish upon a more noble thought, a high point at which your innocence stands supreme.

I managed to achieve my wish and left my thoughts of you in the study with the late afternoon sunlight as if I had been able to put you in a safe place to be taken care of, unsullied by the strivings of my confused human mind, a mechanism so profuse and distracted that it is almost impossible to control, except that one submits to endless years of discipline and training. Most humans prefer to remain prisoners of chaos rather than undertake what seems such a daunting task.

So many humans find serenity elusive. They are hardly given even the briefest taste of it. I am sure that surprises you. For just as you probably cannot imagine the motivations of our elusive minds, so most human beings find it impossible to imagine a state of Light. They are so at odds with themselves that harmony is only a word; an intellectual assumption – and therefore still superficial; or a state experienced mostly only at odd moments during a lifetime and odd moments are so easily forgotten in the clutter of everyday living where the business of survival dictates the mundane nature of their thoughts. Reaching for the stillness in a world so disturbed has to be learned. To teach it is to balance upon a rope in the wind. We are constantly hurled back into the thrashing currents too strong to withstand.

We are caught up in the most desperate struggle, yet know not our own strength. Some of those more in touch with the Creative Force make things which help to induce a state of harmony. Some put musical notes together, some put colours upon canvas, some shape solid materials, some put words on paper, some serve others in hidden, unheeded places, some pour out thought-forms into the ether which lift the human spirit, working unconsciously upon their disseminated consciousness, helping in some small way to make it whole. Each small act of love stops the human race from becoming so sick that it would certainly die.

The few uphold the many.

The many also glimpse the greater glory in moments of surpassing kindliness. But most of them cannot hear the hum of the universe, hear the harmony of the flowers, know the sounds of the symphony of Nature as you could, should you be able to lie in the long grass on a hill, your nose lifted to the breeze, the sunlight warming your black silky fur, making it shine as if it had travelled all those light years especially to single you out – a gleaming dot on the face of a planet caught in dusky clouds.

Stay with me!

Frances closes the book, ties the ribbon and turns to Franziska who is calling with a whispered urgency, forcing her back to the script with trepidation. Will she be able to fulfil that which is required of her, give Franziska the voice she deserves?

December, 1938
I have recorded nothing for so long. I try to remember a little of what has happened. I know too much of those who have thrown themselves from prison windows rather than betray their friends when torture tempted their wearied minds. Instead, I have cherished the shining times with Bertie, Papa and occasionally, Aunt Isabelle.

Once, when I'd had to meet someone across the border, we had three whole days in the mountains. There was snow, white to brilliance in the winter sun and the air was clean and clear and our hearts warm. Bertie and I climbed to a high peak. He held my hand tightly and our faces glowed red and warm as he kissed me with a tenderness so gentle, yet so strong. Later, as we sat beside the flames of a log fire in a candlelit hut, he was silent, far away. I feared he had forgotten me, but then he turned and caught my eye and his face broke into a smile which lit the room as if a thousand candles burned. In his silence he was mourning all that we have lost and may well lose. I believe he sees what will be and then I feared that these moments might contain all of our share of life together, that we may never know endless days where parting has no place.

I have made many journeys for him, the danger meaning little because it is always for him that I take on the risks. He has tried, but could not dissuade me. Bertie calls me 'silver fish' because, he says, I am small and disappear into hidden places before anyone can tell I have been there. The net has often been closed, but I have always slipped through. Now it has become much more dangerous. Papi has insisted I go into hiding. Storm clouds gather.

Herr Hitler has signed a pact of friendship with France . . . ?

Frances reads, re-lives, re-writes, but cannot rest. She paces her room and not knowing distracts her; just as when Joe or her children are away and do not call, anxiety distracts her.

She makes green tea and drinks it until its taste is cloying in her mouth, bitter to her tongue and looks for a peace which evades her.

Chapter 17

It is late in the evening. The family have all gone to bed. The house is quiet. Frances's thoughts go to the dog. He can live quite clearly in her thoughts in this quietude. She feels she is communicating with him mind to mind, soul to soul.

Again, I want to leave you in a beautiful place, contentedly breathing the air with a knowledge unknown to me, happy in the infinite embrace of Mother Nature.

This, I must admit, is for the benefit of us both. Leaving you carefully there may help to keep the evil away from me tonight.

It is very hard, but somehow extremely difficult to maintain such high thoughts before going to bed. She goes to kiss her youngest son and as she leant over his peacefully sleeping body in the darkness, anxiety steals up behind her like a thief, snatching quietly at her peace. Would the world leave him protected and untroubled, especially as things go so deep for him? When she once asked him about animals suffering, although very sad, he had thought for a moment, then quietly said, 'Evil never wins in the end, Mum. Worrying makes it worse.'

Then he had looked down. She had wanted, foolishly, to press him, ask another question. But she didn't.

He had said all he had to say on the matter. It was enough.

It is because he understands so much that she is sometimes afraid for him and yet such understanding also provides great strength. She knows she cannot dictate his life. Just as she cannot alter the course of the many dying on the roadside. Now, she has said it. It was an act of surrender. Perhaps, she thinks, I have been trying to play God with all this worrying and questioning instead of leaving it to the silence of inspiration and the onward current of events.

She feels she has failed yet again. The next morning she wakes with the atmosphere of her troubled dreams still clinging to her consciousness, like the mist which clings to the hills, obscuring them. It is a damp and cloudy day, and just as the air is unclear, so is her mind. Again, she feels oppressed as if isolated from the world, as if she is living in a small patch of unreality which no one can see or understand or wants to know about.

Of course, she knows, it is a prison of her own making.

She did manage to be thankful for waking to the new day, despite the clouded air. It is another of her rules and she does not usually forget this token piece of gratitude for life.

But she can't help thinking how thousands like the rescued dogs all over the world will have woken up in cages, in anticipation of fear and distress or in physical pain and discomfort. If she allows herself, she can live that fear. She can shudder at the clinical smells, feel the nausea tearing at her guts, the blood oozing from her unhealed wounds.

But she stops herself. What is the use of empathy without a constructive end in view? Allowing that indulgence without a solution, she could only ever add to the well of suffering and make alleviation more difficult.

She knows it is far better, by imagination, to lift them all up and set them free. Strength lies in loving detachment, while sentimentality is but shallow emotion and serves no useful purpose. I should be stricter with my emotions. If they control, power is lost; if we control, power is gained.

It is because the human species has lost the communion which your species has never lost that it must look for a way through gods, saints and books of their teachings. Yet none of these can deliver the Truth to them, pristine, untainted, assimilable. It is only through the regaining of Communion that we will find it. If only we looked, your kind could teach it to us, but the humility and self-surrender that this demands is anathema to all but the most enlightened among our kind.

We are afraid that if we surrender the self, we will fall into a dark void and be lost forever, whereas your kind lives the words of the man in the great book: *In whose service is perfect freedom.*

Your race serves without question. You have been forced into a damnable slavery which lays a curse upon mankind.

As I wrote those lines, and was about to abandon my scratching pen moving its way across the gaping white pages demanding its words, sunlight broke through the clouds and split into an array of brilliant shafts which seemed to touch this very window to the table on which I write. I may have been dreaming, but it compels me to continue: it is as if we cannot be at peace until the story is told. Perhaps the eye of God himself looked down and said, 'Speak for one of mine'.

That thought has brought back to mind my dream of last night. I was reaching for you, but could not touch you. You were motionless as if not really alive. There was a chain around your neck.

The more I tried to reach out, the more I was mocked by a crowd of people who laughed, pushed, shouted and sneered behind and all around me. The air was grey and dark, a murky green. And then the scene changed; I had to climb some crumbling steps up to a bridge upon which you stood, silent, unmoving, still with a chain about your neck. I reached the bridge. It was very narrow and swayed as I stepped upon it. It was hung high over a gorge. Below gushed a swift, dark river. I did not reach you before I woke.

This afternoon, I will return to these pages. In the intervening hours, I will attend to letters, telephone calls, files full of papers – the paraphernalia of human life.

But first, I will take my own five dogs for a walk. They wait so expectantly for this daily ritual which is for them as new, special and exciting as it was on the very first day. If only we could live so freely in the present moment, unhampered by useless drifting thoughts of past and future, neither of which we can change except by living correctly in the present moment. But I cannot help adding that I will wish that you were with us enjoying the damp sweetness of the pine woods. I cannot help that wishing will bring a tingling behind my eyes and a lump, hard to swallow, in my throat. I will run with the dogs and try and give it to the air.

I will run dressed in a skirt printed bright with full-blown roses for summer bounty, but the brambles will catch at it and dark earth will stain its hem where the grass cannot grow. I'll care but not care. There's a wicked wind blowing. Wicked like the world.

I do not except myself, Dear Dog, for I have not learned the art of forgiveness as you, for forgiveness is more than forgetting – it is forgetting mixed with love, a giving before. It is through you that I am seeking to learn this art. Do I ask too much of your weary spirit? I too, am weary with these momentous questions to which there are never immediate answers, because through human weakness, I hold back, unable to slough away the dross from a self which longs – sometimes, it appears, in vain.

So please forgive me. Help me to be strong in the face of my own weaknesses.

There's a lightness in the sky this morning. The clouds are white and move swiftly in strong air currents across the sun, which appears and disappears by turns.

Jack and Harry have a half day holiday today. Frances says she will drive in and fetch them at lunchtime – the bus goes into town and back only once a day. They run off out of the door and down the gravel driveway, two of the dogs running excitedly with them.

Almost five hours later, Frances pulls up to the school beside the cathedral. Two long faces stare at her – the crowd has long dispersed.

'You're late –'

'I'm starving – we've been waiting for ages.'

'I'm sorry,' she says. 'Really sorry.' What she can't say is, 'I stepped out of time.' She's trying to be there, trying to pin herself to time, but can't say this to two young boys who've been waiting for fifty minutes.

'I'll take you out to lunch, right now,' she says, smiling. 'Chuck your bags in the car – where would you like to go?'

She's afraid of slicing into the afternoon. She's afraid of upsetting her sons. She wants them to be happy. Time, when you are bound to it, always seems to be running out.

I am bound to time and cannot fly. The thought dogs her as she smiles cheerfully and leads two hungry boys to their favourite café. This is freedom, she thinks. Choice. The thought is light and a passing stranger smiles at her. But Franziska walks in her shadow and anxiety tugs at her cheerfulness. It won't let go.

Chapter 18

February, 1939
I am living in a compartment of an attic. This is a new experience. I am learning the art of patience, but oh so slowly. It is cold and I wrap a blanket tightly around myself, but do not get warm. It is deadening to be imprisoned all day, even voluntarily. The decision was taken in an emergency. I could not refuse. But I have books – many books. They take me into worlds beyond this small place so crowded by my presence.

An old friend of Mama's who refuses to direct plays for the Nazis offered his attic as a safe place. I had to accept – the net was closing too fast. His wife, Lola, is an actress, still working. It isn't easy for her, but she sparkles and loves to shine, no matter who her audience is. Her large bosom moves with her laughter. She shouts, laughs and cries by turns, her life swaying on constantly turning tides of powerful emotions. The sounds drift up to me here, a comfort. At first, Gerhardt did not want to tell Lola that I was here. But we had no choice – this is her house too. I trust them with my life. Their child, however, knows nothing of me; I creep around the back stairs when he sleeps.

March, 1939
I hear much that goes on in this house. Anton, a young actor often visits. There is something in his loud voice which disturbs me. Gerhardt is too good to see darkness in any friend and Lola is busy bubbling. Sometimes, in the darkness of the night, when everyone sleeps, I hear Anton's laughter like a character upon a stage, a mask upon his face, laughing, unreal. Laughing, and I am trapped in an attic for safekeeping. I think perhaps Anton likes men, not women, and this will create difficulties for him with the SS. I hear a hollow weakness in him and

silently call 'beware' to my friends. Who knows what thumbscrews may be turned in these times?

I call to Bertie before sleep comes and fly to him in my dreams. My soul goes searching across the night sky. Sometimes I wake knowing the search has not been in vain. And then no walls hold me and I am joy.

I have not seen him for six months and know nothing of his whereabouts. After the big scare, we scattered and hid, each in our holes. I know his not getting in touch has been a decision to protect me, but my heart aches. Should the worst ever happen, should he not live, I should not want to live. Of that, I am certain. I stayed for him and for all that he stands for and should he die, then my life shall not linger as a shadow of something which was once a light.

Frances is lost in the words she places like a jigsaw upon the page. Small miracles called coincidences found the missing pieces of the story she now rewrites for the images which will reclaim one who could not disappear in the sea of shadows.

Almost a week has passed.

Numbness. A hole as large as a cave gapes in her solar-plexus. And no light shines in this dark. The call came half an hour ago. The papers have arrived. They, too, have brought the news.

Rik has been arrested.

The dogs have been returned.

This means that they will be killed. They will all be killed.

The inquisitors, ice-cold, watched unrepentant heretics burn, and they smiled. The laboratory incinerators are modern and efficient.

They will not keep them. But they will not let them remain free. They are stolen property; possessions to be retrieved, but no longer wanted. That they were certainly stolen from the streets or even urban gardens, that they were commandeered in the interests of what passes for science, means nothing. It is only ever the trick of remaining undetected or the deviousness which protects the forever unpunished which counts. In the interests of science, there will be a sacrifice of life.

In the interests of the Holy Church, innocent, everyday people were dragged from their homes. Torture and death were necessary to bring souls unto a loving Jesus, and the Heavens wept. Jesus wept.

Words begin to spill from me. Sorrow cannot be contained. Is today Black Dog's last day? We failed. We failed all five of them. Now their lives will be sucked out of them. Poisoned, and put into black plastic bags to be burned.

Like a thief in the daylight he comes. White-coated, he covers his blackness as life after life he claims. The mask of a sheep, his words – 'Your benefit.' 'Your children's health.' 'Your safety' – betray him. All terrible lies to hide the blackness of his heart.

Vanity. Vanity, your name is Man and Pride your poisoned sire. I am wearing a white dress to clean the heavy atmosphere.

Spotless soft cotton, spotless black dog. Soft warmth made cold. I do not want to speak to anyone not of the immediate family. My husband must answer the telephone's incessant bell. He must also be the receiver of all sorrows today and not complain. Dizzily, I sink into a downward spiral, looking for a light which does not exist. I look to hide away in sleep which will not cover me. I lie on cold stone to escape the cushioned comfort of my existence. Soon the leaves will fall and the world will be stark and cold. The moon is made of dust.

Not even a grave. Fire will consume the body without ceremony. The entire ceremony will be my thoughts struggling through the fog of angered, hollowed, nauseous weeping.

Today Death has dominion.

First came deductions; later came the facts. Garbled, hearsay at first. What is certain is that the van was traced. Pinkie knew whose car would be involved in the documents raid. It was her husband, Steve, who was arrested. He has often admitted fear of arrest, fear of pressure which he could not withstand. A trade-off? A car, its description, its number?

Rik may well have kept them overnight, afraid of risking a long drive after closing-time, when he could be stopped. He had a long drive, was probably stopped on the way; the description circulated. Too easy.

They did not know. They thought they were betraying papers, and people, of course.

They did not know that the price was the lives of five dogs. Have they heard? They must know by now.

But they are silent. How is it inside that silence?

How is it that the three, all vegans – a non-violent diet their professed lifestyle, now have lives, or rather, deaths on their hands?

I ask, that is all.

Joe comes to her with tea, sets it down, and asks her to join him on the old chaise longue she inherited from her great aunt. The way she puts her hand on it as she sits says everything about her love for its faded velvet shabbiness, its warm, sagging, uneven springs which speak of a life lived usefully, the reassurance it supplies, imbued as it is with its owner's warmth.

But as Joe sits, he complains, 'You should get this thing repaired or get rid of it.' His values are not hers. She looks at him from the depths of her despair with something like scorn in her eyes. 'The springs have gone.' He offers and shrugs. 'Well, it's up to you.'

She nods and turns away.

'Come on,' he says. 'Have some tea with me.'

He puts his arm around her shoulder.

'It's hard,' he says.

She sees there are almost tears in his eyes and is surprised. She hears him. 'I don't know how to help you. Except by being here.'

During the following days, she turns away when Joe creeps into her room where the curtains are permanently drawn. She won't eat, can't. She hears him call friends; she doesn't care that he's talking about her, but she won't brook any interference, won't let him tell her what she should be doing or feeling. She knows he doesn't really know her and she knows there's a dark layer of anger under this depression which has confused her, like a frightened rabbit hiding in its burrow from the hunter's gun. But she and her attacker are one. It lives inside her, too terrifying to allow into the light. She is left alone. Finally Joe comes and arranging his face before he speaks, which tells her how he feels the risk, says, 'There is something more.' His insights, again, she thinks. Remarkable.

She stares at him with a look that tells him she wants to speak, but can't.

'You have to tell me,' he says. 'We all need to know. What's happened with this dog has touched something deeper.'

She allows questioning surprise on to her face to tell him he's right. 'They're pushing for this script,' she says.

'Don't be a victim,' he almost pleads. 'Don't stop taking action. It's the only way out.' He pushes her to take a shower, to change her clothes, put on something bright. He's bought a rosebush for the dog and got a man in the village to carve a small stone.

'Get changed and we'll plant the bush by the stone and I'll take you out to lunch.'

She can't resist this insistence. Has he been talking to a woman? Frances wonders to herself. She smiles a little as he gently squeezes her shoulder before leaving the room.

She does as instructed, the process almost automatic, doing her best to block thought. She pulls on a bright pink fitted dress and steps into flat black shoes.

Out in the garden, the sun is shining through fast-moving clouds as a brisk autumn wind begins too soon to relieve the trees of their leaves.

The leaves must fall.

Frances crouches to look at the stone on which is carved:

Tears fell for me
And all the sons and daughters of my Father's house.

Tears fall upon Frances's face as they plant the white rose and think of the gardens of paradise.

She can't eat lunch, but drinks sparkling wine as they sit in the garden of their local pub. Joe puts a hand on hers across the table. At the same moment, a black Labrador leaves its owner and runs up to Frances, sits and lifts its paw to her knee. She puts a hand on its head. Called away, it turns, looks in the direction of the call, turns back, makes a small sound as if asking for something, then goes, obeying the call.

'What was he saying?' Joe smiles. Frances sighs, overcome with emotion.

'My father,' she says. 'You know he was a doctor, that he did research. I've never told you that when I was just sixteen, I discovered he used animals. I went to meet him at work. We were going out. I was waiting in the office. He was late coming through. It was a big teaching hospital. I went looking for him – no one saw me, no one stopped me. I found him, this apparently charming man. When he saw me, looking at what he was doing, he shouted, 'Get out!' I turned and ran and ran. We didn't go out together. I never wanted to see him again. I went to live with my aunt. My mother was a simple sort of woman. Unquestioning. I don't think she'd ever realised exactly what he was doing. She understood how I felt. She never tried to force me to come back. She just accepted my decision. I think she felt horribly guilty. I wouldn't speak to him, wouldn't see him. I hated him from that day.

He died six months later – a heart attack – and I'd never spoken to him again, only hated him for what he'd been doing. I was glad when he died. Glad when my father died.'

'I knew you didn't get on with him,' Joe says. 'I presumed he'd got heavy-handed, jealous of you growing up -'

Frances slowly shakes her head, then her voice brightens.

'I looked in on the funeral for my mother's sake. I dressed in the brightest red I could find – scarlet. All those stuffy, superior colleagues of his looked askance, but I almost skipped through them to my mother's side. She was a new woman when he'd gone. She blossomed. She met another man the following year. I stayed on with her sister until I was eighteen. I can still hear the dogs' whimpering in his laboratory. I am so ashamed of him. I pleaded with my mother to tell me I was another man's child. I could only think of him as a cold-blooded murderer –'

They walk home slowly and spend the rest of the afternoon talking, examining the ghost. Joe offers no answers, no explanations, only saying, 'He obviously felt guilty'. He listens, asks questions and waits; she knows he hopes to help her rid herself of the miasma she calls, 'The foul stain of my father'.

The children are pleased to find their mother looking almost like herself again at dinner that night. The following morning, a chink of light let into the musty cupboard of her past allows her to return to her work.

Chapter 19

Late September, 1939
In Berlin. Leaves were falling as leaves must fall, their silent fluttering whispering 'winter comes', one by one, yellow ochre, sienna, crimson, burgundy, sepia, calling, calling 'winter comes'.

I have kept a resigned calm, hidden away between stifling, sloping walls these long months, kept sane by nurturing my dreams, kept alive by chance messages from Pauli. I live from one day to the next, thoughts are my only freedom, dreams are my only release, where visions shift with reality and keep me hovering between two worlds. Heaven and Hell, enclosed in a shell, like a moth, saved from the flame, fluttering between cupped hands.

Night. The silence is shattered.

There is a loud banging on the door at four o'clock in the morning. I was awake and alert, every nerve tensed at the first knock. It could only mean one thing. I shook uncontrollably, reaching for my clothes. It was a huge effort; a nightmare where my limbs refused to move to the command of my will. Buttons slipped through my shaking fingers and would not fit into their holes. Four times I tried. More banging on the door. My breath came shallow and too quickly. I forgot to breathe. My lungs hurt. I gasped for air like the drowning. Adrenaline flooded me, made my head light, too light to think. My feet will not move. The cold cramped my muscles. The pain vied with the giddiness.

Shouting.

The shouting grew louder as I was sucked into a vortex of terror. My thoughts flew to the child asleep in his room. I called on God and uttered Bertie's name to give me courage. Should they be arrested, I must not hide and save myself. I know their ways better than they do. Lola will not survive this. Gerhardt can be strong, silent. Lola's screams pierced the air. Lola was hysterical, screaming and weeping by turns.

I wanted to burst out, stand with them. More banging. Heavy steps on the stairs. I could not breathe. Shouted commands:

'Get the child out of bed!'

I wanted to shout. I put a hand over my mouth. What is best? My body shook violently, no longer my own.

'Get downstairs!' They are shouting at Lola who protests, screaming for her child. Gerhardt's voice is quiet.

I put my ear to the wooden panel.

Odd words: Gerhardt's voice: 'There's nothing here.'

'We decide that! Do you think we don't know the lies you types come up with?'

'Nothing, I tell you!' Gerhardt has courage.

The Gestapo don't listen to people. They stamp on them.

The stamping grows fainter. Gone to another part of the house.

I reached for a blanket to stop the shivering. It increased. My knuckles were clenched, white against the dark grey wool in the darkness. Every muscle was locked.

Bertie's broken face. Cells in underground corridors. Locked doors. No windows. Shouting. Laughter.

Bertie's broken face. Thoughts stop.

Stomping. Heavy boots. A voice. Cold. Loud. Inevitable. A kick. The panel splits, but I am still hidden.

I was sure I could hear Anton's voice echoing behind the shouts and screams, his mask nodding as the wooden panel split to reveal me, this small dark girl wrapped in a woollen blanket. Lola could not help herself. One word, a look in an unguarded moment and Anton had guessed. It gave him a hand to play in a game where fear dictated the rules.

The Gestapo were everywhere, snooping in bars and restaurants, hanging around the theatre. One night they entered by the stage door, marched into his dressing room. They ordered him to entertain them, a drag queen upon the stage, playing to an empty theatre after dark. They told him he was *Dreck*, dirt to be swept away, but then a crack opened in the door which threatened to close upon him. What could he tell them of others? He stumbled in his high heels. Queen Anton ordered to flaunt herself. They laughed in the empty theatre in the darkness and a spotlight shone on Anton's lips painted scarlet to kiss.

'He knew more didn't he?' They laughed, hollow, echoing laughter. And their faces were masks in the dark.

Anton's mascara ran in dirty little rivulets down his white cheeks when they left him, trembling, prostrate upon an empty stage. Gerhardt was already in their sights. A word, some small excuse was all they needed to put the spark to the firecracker. They twisted arms with clever lies, reading their subjects' weaknesses by methods centuries old: Torquemada's minions still pace a kingdom of tentacled evil which refuses to die because man has not yet conquered that part of him which bows to the monarch of the Dark. Someone from the theatre warned Gerhardt of what had happened.

That Gerhardt and Lola should be dragged outside into the darkness where the cold bit into their flesh was horror enough to Franziska; that their eight-year-old son should be taken screaming from his bed, was too much for her to bear. With a strength called up from subconscious deeps, I wanted to break out and fling protesting arms about the child but I was frozen rigid.

Hours later, Gerhardt wept like a baby, when he was free and they were gone. Silence sealed him. Silence saved him – and his theatrical skill, quick intelligence and strength of will. These facilitated his escape. He searched day and night and vain was the search for the sparkle of his life which ended with the morning of that day. He told me it was Anton who had betrayed them. Anton told him just how it had happened and now he has been taken away. There was no reward.

I told him I must go away. I was putting him in danger. He said he was going to search for them and left me alone. The next night, they came again. He was not there and so they broke the door, crashed into the house and they found me. Had they found Gerhardt? Had Lola told them in exchange for their child? I can never know. They were good to me. I scream when the hand that came crashing down upon the left side of my face sent me spinning to the ground. I was dragged away. I hoped Gerhardt was safe.

Dear Dog, Frances, sitting in her study, feels the blow, is stunned. Is Franziska here with her? Was she once Franziska in a previous personality? What is this resonance? She remains stunned, for a full ten minutes or so and waits for it to pass.

Dear Dog, I have told you of a Great One who came to live among humankind to teach by his loving sacrifice. There is one line in the story told by one who followed him. It describes the time of his persecution and attempted murder by those who could not comprehend his Light. He foresaw the murder of His teaching by those who would betray them. This line has been described as one full of 'ineffable pathos'. It is: *Jesus wept.*

This did not happen but once. Because, as he told, he was at one with all things in His love.

That moment lives time and again. In that moment when I stopped and looked, I saw it in your eyes, that pristine essence which is the Creator in you, and I felt greatly ashamed of my human frailty. I can only suppose that, by addressing all of this to you, I am seeking an expiation.

Such thoughts make anger stir in me again – no doubt it is anger with myself, I must share in the collective guilt of the human race, finding a way through trial and error.

The evening closes in now and the night will soon offer its dreams and should the fear enfold me, forsake me, protect yourself from the grim places of man's unkindness. For I know there are planes of the lost ones, planes of man's making, and if it is for me to wander there as an inevitable consequence, it surely is not for you. Your sacrifice is done. We can only ever make our own sacrifice. Did your soul volunteer or was it their terrible inversion of truth which took you? They kill and call it sacrifice. The world is overturned. We must wait for the dawn when a new horizon, bright with promise, will awaken our souls. Withdraw, for sometimes as the evening spreads its dark cloak upon the earth, I am overcome with my own shadow and must search for the inner light.

I put your face aside in case the memories of what must be written should stir a hatred which would bring a fear or a sorrow too deep which would bring despair, for these are the stuff of human ways and not, at this time, for you to share. If I must weep in my own wilderness, it must be alone.

Another day.

Frances saw Black Dog last night. He came in a dream and she was troubled.

Joe brought her a huge bunch of roses from the garden, white for purity and pink for love. The second crop, grown on after summer's dead heads were snapped clean away. They die and come again bringing eternal hope, life renewed.

She is going to light a candle in a human place of worship, for humans and for creatures. She returns to write to Black Dog.

Many of us find it hard to go on living here knowing how it is for those like you still left behind, wretched, terrified. Perhaps I am envious of you now that you have gone before.

Perhaps when I fall into sleep, I long to follow you and not to wake again into this dangerous place. You see, sometimes I have seen the so-called dead creatures still dear, in the freedom of sleep, and waking, have longed to retrieve the sights, the touch, the contact, the love made visible, so much stronger there.

They honour me with such loving return. But you and I, we still have something to do. I must give you your freedom by not envying it. There are different paths for all of us and yours and mine have crossed. When will the night yield more of her secrets? That very thought opens the floodgates again – you see it was people who had no idea how to control their emotions and had lost their hearts along the way who allowed your death.

I am sure that this must puzzle you a great deal, because in you there was no conflict, no self-seeking, no thought of revenge, only a friendliness which I have to call love and a deep, pitying, sadness.

Numbness. Life has become a blur. Time has passed. Dark winter months have enclosed me, but now recede.

That is your story. The feelings aroused by the treachery of those three were so strong that I was afraid to write them down. Such feelings are not for shaping into any form of physical reality. They were already too threatening on the plane where they existed, surviving in emotional anarchy and I, allowing myself to be influenced by their misrule.

I could not find it in me to forgive, and my world was peopled by reflections. I have lived in misery, thrashing about pointlessly in a sea of suffering. A self-made sea, which stretched to a far horizon, misty, occluded, oppressive. The winter settled like a heavy, wet cloak and beneath it, I shivered, alone. Very little good could reach me in such a state. I became weaker and illness struck three times. Twice, I blamed the three: your captors, your killers and all those who stand by and do not want to know; those who know, yet idle, do nothing, and even those who do something, but remain hopelessly ineffective. I accused thousands when my sick thoughts travelled out and scurried back to me, pushing me over, pulling me under, until I was drowning. Salt sea tears engulfed me and lived behind my eyes, filled my head. Clean white sheets threatened me. Sleep sometimes blotted out and healed awhile, sometimes offering too much of itself, it terrified me. No hand could touch me, for I turned away with silent screams. I lived on the edge of darkness and there was no escape. I was my own tormentor. Break open the rock of pain and you will find precious treasure within.

Your peace. Tranquillity had become a word whose meaning was lost; it lived only in the tarnished memories of past sunsets, the fantasy dreams of adolescence and the perfumed bloom of yellow roses lost in a childhood all but forgotten.

Through a feverish delirium, I lost myself and having laid a request for redemption, came back with a new mind and, step by step, began to retrieve love and newness.

Former quarrels and dissent were far removed and lived apart from me. Their shadowy influence had left.

New impetus has come with the beginning of spring and like a tender shoot, must be nurtured against the storms which always threaten. It lives, growing invisibly, in a time not of our construction. Its minutes cannot be ticked and its days cannot be numbered.

Chapter 20

Dear Dog, I hear that Rik is to be released from prison today. Six months, less remission for good behaviour, of claustrophobic gloom will not follow him into the sunlight. Unceasingly mindful of the suffering of your kind, he cannot bow to self-pity and repels reminders of pain gladly borne. Neither the dangling of steely keys, nor the threatening conspiracy of silence over the evil that is done, will daunt him.

Today has brought other news. Steve Lawton has entered a different prison, that of his own mind. He lives at the moment in a hospital ward, having temporarily withdrawn from what we call reality. His wife had departed some weeks ago, unable to bear his strangeness...

The very drugs he raged against will now be administered to him. That too, is very wrong.

We have woven a web so dangerous; it catches us at every turn. Groping, we are ensnared. We are the spider *and* the fly.

They cannot see this, those to whom the mind's vast uncharted regions remain a mystery which evades their clumsy labelling.

Now ours is the guilt of knowing that we have all fallen into the trap; sunk into the pit so thinly camouflaged. Waiting for release.

As two escape, one more fails. The powers need no henchmen; they need no keys.

We hand them over with our fears and in our darkest moments build our cells in which to hide.

> *We forget the Light.*
> *We forget the love available.*
> *We forget we have the freedom of the universe.*
> *We forget our vision.*
> *We forget, in every misconceived thought, to set you free.*

*We forget that miracles are natural occurrences on other
     planes of being.*

And imagining every kind of limitation, we place obstacles on the road to your Liberation. Others have no power except that which we concede to them.

And all the blind ambition, all the scientific analysis, all the chatter, all the evading, self-deluding processes we suffer, displace the love, which absent, cannot feed us.

We forget that unloving, we wither and we too shall die.

I accept your lesson, Dear Dog, with a heart broken open and waiting. I promise to keep the dream safe and whole within me.

This is ours. Our work. Now that they can never again lay their hands on you.

A cluster of women waited in the chill September dawn, guarded by three overfed SS men. Raindrops falling. Raindrops upon stone. Franziska, twenty-one years old. The storm gathers. Many leaves shall be torn from the tree, but all are numbered. Resigned, she waited, shivering, her eyes kept away from these men whose anger hungered for sustenance.

The journey in the truck was cramped, its stolen cargo overcome by a languor of which they could not speak.

The camp, a pit of evil into which they were thrown, turned each living day into an eternity to be endured, survival of each dark hour a victory of the human spirit.

Franziska, fragile, beautiful, vital, untainted, became a pet to the beasts who would scavenge that which they could not own.

Her innocence, once worshipped by her beloved, was ravaged by a ton of white pork-fed flesh, laughing as it stole the body it could never be given. She screamed, and no one heard.

Dazed, blinded, deafened, numbed, she became an empty vessel. A random child of this savagery took root in her. Weeks of horror passed lest it might own her. But it could not live. On the day it left her, Franziska thanked a merciful Creator. The blood flowed like a river and would not be stopped, carrying her away from her tormentors.

But Franziska was not alone. Her angel did not leave her. A stranger became a friend in this strange place. She scribbled the last words upon scraps of paper in the camp hospital hut as the weakness crept upon Franziska. Smuggled out, this epitaph survived, a song to her life, offered for a vision of a better day.

I walk into a hall of mirrors so cruel they crush me. I arrive like a hero late, long after the battle is finished and seethe in ecstasy silenced before it began to speak.

Worlds are numbered in my name; planets collide and I am torn apart by what I am: divided, like the stars, into millions, yet one with all that feels throughout the living universe all interlaced with darkness too profound and awesome to contemplate. The days of my years are ruins in a memory fit for the blessedness of forgetfulness of old age, yet my youth will not save me. Fire like fever burns my pulses for all the precious stones I threw into the ashes of lost dreams because I had forgotten their value when the gods twirled them in my palms. Ungrateful child, who glimpsed a wild and ordered infinity and chose instead a personal God and has found that He/She cannot be named and all is lost when the vision fades. Like desert sands burnt aeons back and the momentous works of millions are buried in a moment's fitful breeze. Eking out my moments I am starved of the life I know was mine by right and a noble heritage thrown into the dust. I too shall be dust but the glimpses of heaven's despair mirrored on my mind shall not disintegrate with this dead flesh.

Grief lives on in the air to be breathed by the numberless ones who shall live long after me and be sent mad by this same moon which coldly lights my dim shadow now.

I pluck the stars to thread and hang about my neck and set upon my brow and, though naked, cry to my tormentors: 'These are lights electric you can never put out: Tear at me how you will!'

I ate a piece of moon tonight and see a world superimposed upon your wretched vision of a woe begotten hell. My tears burn furrows in your fattened cheeks and your night is all at once put out.

I am transfixed by a thousand dark nights but something will not let them keep me. My fevered mind is a light. The cold tears at my skin as if I were to be torn to pieces inch by inch, each nerve laid raw and biting. It is a sharp and needled cold which knows no mercy and is dumb. My white starlight necklace glints in your demon's bloodshot eyes and you laugh the crazed laugh of evil afraid of itself, carrying high the banner which blazes the insignia of its own destruction. You laugh your blind way into the pit and cannot see its darkness because you are one with it. Every child's scream nails you to your cross, lowers you another notch, another mile into that deep dark void where all is silence and blackness, on towards that most final disintegration, a soul undone.

I sing hymns for you. The funeral has begun because somewhere a light so strong has shone that all the thousand devils must destroy themselves as their natures are revealed.

You cannot pin me with this pain. Another dawn calls me now. Its flares rose in the midnight sky. I have seen all my ugliness and have stepped out of its shabby coat. It is heaped with all those belongings which do not belong.

And so you, who have taken all that which once belonged to us, have taken the burden of our sins and carry them now upon your backs. O nation which gave me birth, ranged around the puppet who acts out all your mad desires! You who took upon yourself this gall of the mighty fallen, the deadliest, the bitterest gall of all.

In your utter greed, you eat up all our rottenness and like maggots which cleanse wounds you have cleansed us now from unknown aeons of sinning.

How free I feel! No longer bound to human bondage. A paradise is mine which gems and flowers and dogs and stars inhabit, moving in the gentle order of a universe ordained by a Creator whose name is Love. My loyalty moves now to that ordinance and I am free to be as I was created. When death comes, I shall be as a bird plucked from a cage that barred my spirit for a thousand years and more. I shall soar to the widest heavens. Who shall come with me? Who, too, shall rise?

Like wild geese, we'll form a wondrous arc across the morning sky.

By what means we shall be jolted from this fleshly form I cannot tell. A veil is drawn across the name of my departing. There are many means arranged – lead shot in a moment through my thinking brain, the passage of sweet air stopped in long gasping minutes by their poisoned gas, ill-met by their batons which crush skulls with all hell's hatred summoned up from the deep pain of ages imprisoned in the night of this earth's soul, or caught in an urgent deranged desire, flying to an elected suicide in the wires which hem us in with their deadly current to burn our blood, flesh cooked in a flash, sizzled, or deep frozen to a stone, like some who will not yield.

All extremes are offered us, so what need to confine our self to this small trap? Its teeth are set and they'll snap without due warning. Too weak for weeping, these blind beggars of my fears wander aimlessly, caught in the tyrant's clutches and they are all the lambs who lay bleeding upon Passover tables and blessed by priests in black and purple robes holding jewel encrusted crosses. Oh wash your hands, my brothers and sisters. All death that was and is, is ours. You sleep too long. I will watch for you a while, but who knows how long until a new day's dawn? My teeth chatter to themselves and ask if I am not mad with hunger.

Is this a frenzy born of threat beyond imagining? But no, I protest against this nagging doubter who comes to torment my soul and tempt it into utter death. They go, but shall not take us on their crooked path, of snakes and scorpions, thorns and sulphured breath. O fetid parts of me be cleansed. I am lightened. I shall fly with my companions.

I know somewhere there is a light which forces this circumstance, a purpose, a resolution of a nightmare which loomed but never shared its ugliness so much as now.

My hope of this light is the beaded dew of dawn's first awakening upon an eternal field all glittering emerald, renewed every living minute. There is no fading of the rays, but an infinite inherent light. No shadow stalks that place.

Immortal Aurora, touch us with your rosy fingers, and waken this beggarly company in the name of Love from the sleep which stole us from Eden in a time which memory fails to reach.

My few years are eclipsed in the cleansing fire of pain, when pride had manufactured tinselled dreams of splendour. This false light flickers weakly now, spattering amidst its own grey dust.

Evil has come, but woe to those through whom it has come for they shall fail because we do not answer to their names for us.

Rather have we named them and the white dove, its wings outstretched, hovers, a silent companion, a sign until the end of time of the stillness of peace amidst swirling planets born and destroyed, a vast breathing universe, a heaven resting in the palm of the Creator's hand.

I breathe its breath but lightly now and whatever element shall lay the last hand upon this broken face shall be a brother-sister in the final hour. The sky awaits me! Aurora's silent song is spirit full to bursting with this pink breath and all is glorious stillness.

We shall step lightly now, for Freedom comes.

When Gerhardt sat beside Aunty Isabelle's fire with his son, having returned from Switzerland in 1947, the snow outside wrapped a beautiful silence about his torment. The three, staring into the crackling flames, were speechless survivors upon the wasteland of a battlefield, staggering with wounds which even the balm of Isabelle's loving wisdom could not heal. Pauli's group had made it possible for Gerhardt and his son to escape, but Lola had disappeared. Those loved lay dead about them as if the room itself were the wasteland and all the white, white falling snow could not cleanse the earth of its stains, nor its silence hush the weeping for the dead still dying over and over in the grief of those who loved them.

Chapter 21

Frances steps over the fence. The dogs slip under it, sliding through spaces which look too small for their bodies. While Lord Cecil Llewellyn jumps over the stone wall, and Mr Collins follows with a great leap of joy. She runs across the sloping field, once a parkland to this country house, runs against the wind, a spattering of rain hitting her face with the gentleness of dewdrops. She runs to be free, to cleanse away cloying history, to be free so that Franziska's story can live a life of its own now. The dogs are barking, skipping, leaping over streams and broken branches scattered by recent winds. They run into the woodland. She leans against an aged tree, longs for its strength, its watchful knowingness. It has seen centuries pass and greened to each new springtime renewed.

'Renew my soul!' comes as an involuntary incantation vibrating through her heated brain. This task has not been easy – rain has become for her the soaking kind which made mud to increase the suffering of the millions trapped in hell's maw; cold has become the killing kind which froze bodies beyond endurance or brought the dying to the brink; shouting has become the evil kind sounded by passions risen from the primeval dark and in the night hours she has seen their wicked laughter feeding greedily upon the relentless suffering as if all life must, like a light, be snuffed out, helpless against the gushing tide of blackness. Frances has lived among the faceless ones; dissolved the mirage of time.

All tides return. Love and gifts and harm and thoughts and spring flowers return, all after their kind.

Only love can break the harm and feel the flowers and give good gifts.

All things are connected.

Frances runs again along the path between the trees. Franziska held her dream and lived with a vision of angels, yet she was heedless of her life.

Frances has seen her death.

The ground is sloping, the moss is a brilliant, luminescent green, damp upon buried stones.

Frances slips and falls. She calls out in pain and shock. Franziska is dead! How could she survive, heedless, entwined by a love, enchanted by another self which led her into the unknown?

Dead. With all that was beautiful in her crushed to a bloodied pulp as if a lighted, slender innocence would be a threat most terrible to the dark, inrushing tide.

Frances feels her legs crumpled beneath her; her face is bruised. She is shaken and cannot stand. The wood is quiet. The dogs are panting, waiting, anxious, waiting.

Frances has felt the assault upon her own body. Her face twists involuntarily to one side. The whole of the left side of her face is a bloodied mess; a gaping hole. The whip, she's seen it, knows its every detail; the large hand with killer's strength, she's felt it.

Everything is fragile at this moment. Branches are bare. There is no strength to stand. There is nothing of her own to grasp. A dog whimpers.

She was thrown, still beautiful, a waxen image of that one so 'lovely, pure and fair', upon a heap of bodies and covered, the heavy earth stealing the little that was left of breath to keep her in that place of all horrors, choking the last wisps from the throat which had spoken words as beautiful as flowers, their petals crushed.

It was all robbed. As a thief in the night they came and took the innocence by deadly force, laughing in the act. Robbing by day, they took what was lovely, what was fair, but the purity lay beyond their reach. She breathed another air than theirs. She saw another world and they sought to conquer it by killing her sight. But she could not fade. As the light died to her eyes, she woke into another day and waited, her vision not dead, where time has no meaning, for an exorcism.

There must be a cleansing for reparation, for restoration. Frances, still upon the ground, hears Franziska's voice, calling, not weak or afraid, but clear as the birdsong in this damp wood, calling out across that space where yesterday is not lit by a noonday sun and tomorrow already is, because it is of this bright, insistent moment.

It calls, 'Finish! In the grand finale, you will hear the herald! A new time comes!'

Franziska had laid herself upon the sacrificial altar and the men of shadows had laughed at the taking of this pure life which could not comprehend their living death.

There was still breath in her as they dragged her away. She withdrew from the anguish and horror staring in the eyes of those who could not save her and thought only of God and her beloved, called 'Bertie, Papa, Mama, Isabelle', as if they were a company together summoned by a power beyond them to travel this weary road, to gather now at this cross-road as one was pushed away. The earth, heavy upon her chest, the earth thrown upon her broken face, Mother Earth engulfed her, sucked her breath away.

It was Bertie's hand stretched out as her spirit rose, smiling, both blue eyes shining, alight with joy to find her.

Pauli, Lisalotte and Isabelle survived to mourn. Pauli's resistance work took his health; his life ended in the early fifties. Lisalotte later married again and lived into the seventies.

Isabelle is a very old lady, still beautiful, her eyes still shine. She lives alone in the country amidst the heavy oak and mahogany furniture, pieces which look as if they will last forever; the elaborate carvings on the chest, the heavy perfumed smell of polish, the glow from the fire and the heavy curtains keeping the cold outside. She will survive to see her darling child live again and will smile with contentment to know how she encouraged that young love which neither the darkest evil nor the mightiest tyranny could break.

Epilogue

Frances begins filming *Franziska*. The young actress is perfect for the part. She speaks every word as if it were her own. Her features, her body, become Franziska's. Years have parted like waves and through her, Franziska walks in all her light and majesty, alive and bright, in love with life. Time has melted. Space cannot be measured. All is well.

Frances watches, humbled by this gift. The grave could not hold this spirit. It flew and found her and now it touches her, Franziska and Bertie as if by magic. She has come to tell that love is life, and death, though one in millions, is not departing, and life cannot be lived in vain.

'Franziska!' Frances calls across the terraces in the twinkling darkness – 'Franziska, your name was not written in water. Your name is written in the stars.' You sing aloud for all the unsung heroes, whose lives, great in the heavens, were invisible upon this small planet, scattered among the ashes of the fire which consumed their loves and dreams. Each one is counted, each one numbered, each one named.

Joe is writing the requiem which shall bring a thousand souls to peace. And they shall be exalted. He stands behind her now in silent wonder.

Who were Franziska and Bertie? Who are we?

Their mystery is a secret hinted at in the music he hears. It is a Gloria. The voices swell in the night's filled silence. They are not alone.

Frances enters a new day where wonders call.

Dear Dog, the dreams of you told our story. The unfolded events for me to mend the time.

Today the wild daffodils have broken their sunshine into the meadow, each yellow petal straining its call to the breeze which rocks their hollowed stems.

I am wakening too, and I call out for all to know that the theft of life and happiness of one kind can never return as healing to another. How can we give back the millions of lives which have been stolen? Answer me, Dear Dog, in some still moment, answer this most terrible of questions. Out walking in the wood I called again this morning, called into the air. Following a streak of silver in the sky, I fixed my eyes upon the distant light which seemed to call me through the narrow avenue along the firs. And then the sky took on shapes I had never seen before. The faces of animals came, one following upon another, until, disintegrating into the blueness, they let me go once more.

I am compelled to speak for you. Now you have finished our story. How shall I write of your last gift, so immense, yet momentary?

Eyes heavy, drowsy, I drifted from wakefulness upon the sofa in my study this afternoon and lightly suspended as between two worlds, a meeting took place.

Whole and gleaming, brown eyes sparkling, your fur as if it had been brushed with silk, you appeared.

As I looked into your face, there was a joy to end all sorrows.

I returned to the world, sad at our parting, yet certain in the knowledge that you live in no valley of shadows.

We have overcome an evil.

Together we found the freedom of the universe where time and space are not.

We have found the place of Wholeness, where all becomes One, and your story, reaching out to many, with love, will take them a little nearer to that place where longing ends. To that place where no darkness can occlude the everlasting Light and where Life is never cut off, but simply changed from glory into Glory.

I fear we may be parted now awhile, until the place where years pass as minutes, uncounted, is mine to enter. Until I can reach that space which you have found, where love makes no demands, but is of itself renewed. You were tattooed with numbers and yet you are dear and named.

Dear Dog, Franziska, every hair on your head is numbered. We will not forget.

Dear Dog, Franziska in Memoriam, let these words from a Normandy crucifix of 1632 be yours.

> *I Am The Great Sun, but you do not see me, I am your husband, but you turn away.*
>
> *I am the captive, but you do not free me, I am the captain you will not obey.*
>
> *I am the truth, but you will not believe me, I am the city where you will not stay,*
>
> *I am your wife, your child, but you will leave me, I am that God to whom you will not pray.*
>
> *I am your counsel, but you do not hear me, I am your lover whom you will betray,*
>
> *I am the victor, but you do not cheer me, I am the holy dove whom you will slay.*
>
> *I am your life, but if you will not name me,*
> *Seal up your soul with tears, and never blame me.*